THE ADVENTURES OF
MICHAEL MacINNES

JEFF CARNEY

FARRAR, STRAUS AND GIROUX
NEW YORK

Copyright © 2006 by Jeff Carney
All rights reserved
Distributed in Canada by Douglas & McIntyre Ltd.
Printed in the United States of America
Designed by Barbara Grzeslo
First edition, 2006
1 3 5 7 9 10 8 6 4 2

www.fsgkidsbooks.com

Library of Congress Cataloging-in-Publication Data
Carney, Jeff.
    The adventures of Michael MacInnes by Jeff Carney.— 1st ed.
        p.   cm.
    Summary: In 1924, high school junior Michael MacInnes, a free-thinking
poet and orphaned scholarship student, stirs up trouble when he challenges
the rules and traditions of his prep school.
    ISBN-13: 978-0-374-30146-0
    ISBN-10: 0-374-30146-8
    [1. Boarding schools—Fiction. 2. Schools—Fiction. 3. Nineteen
twenties—Fiction. 4. Orphans—Fiction. 5. Poets—Fiction.] I. Title.

PZ7.C21777 Ad 2006
[Fic]—dc22

2004057669

For Russ

THE ADVENTURES OF
MICHAEL MacINNES

1

Mad, bad, and dangerous to know.

—LADY CAROLINE LAMB

Roger Legrande rode the train to Stoney Batter one hot September morning in 1924. Hot? It was miserable. Roger had worn his best wool suit, and the car was as sultry as an oven. As the train steamed into the foothills of western Maryland, sweat soaked his stockings and puddled in his shoes. Still, he suffered the heat in silence. He didn't dare make a bad impression on opening day.

"Gosh, I could use a drink," a voice next to him said. The speaker, a boy Roger's age, had spent most of the trip reading a book of poetry with the name Byron on the cover. He snapped the book shut and pulled a silver-plated flask from his trouser leg. "Want some?" he said to Roger.

"Is it cold?"

"Not very."

"Hmm." Roger licked the sweat from his upper lip. "Is it wet?"

"Absolutely."

"I *am* a bit thirsty," he confessed.

The boy smiled and stuck out his hand. "Michael MacInnes, class of '26. I'm new this year."

Roger relaxed. He'd been sure he was the only new boy aboard.

"Roger Legrande. Looks like we're in the same class."

They shook hands like reunited friends.

"Here's to a speedy train ride." MacInnes sipped from the flask and gave it to Roger.

Roger took it, and before he knew what was happening he'd belted down three blistering mouthfuls of what must have been, could only have been—

"Hey!" he gasped. "That's—"

"Keep it down!" MacInnes cut him off. "I thought you knew."

"How would I know?"

"I told you it was wet, didn't I?"

"I thought you meant wet like water, not wet like whiskey."

"Just trying to be a chum."

"Some chum," Roger said. "I could get thrown out of school just for *talking* to the likes of you. There's a Prohibition on, you know."

MacInnes seemed genuinely surprised.

"Do you think they take all that stuff seriously?"

"Haven't you heard? The Dean Reverend beats lawbreakers with a wooden paddle. I hear he almost killed a fellow once."

"No kidding?"

MacInnes scratched the stubble on his jaw. He was a handsome enough boy, if a bit unrefined, with sharp blue eyes and a shock of auburn hair that splashed over his collar like a bohemian's.

"Well," he said, "if we're going to be prisoners, we might as well enjoy our last moments of freedom." He returned the flask to his trousers and fished two cigars from his suit coat. "Join me?"

Roger glanced around. The car was filled with Stoney Batter boys. Some read quietly, some played cards, some talked about the interhouse rivalry between Craxton and Marshall, the two campus dormitories. A handful of masters and their wives occupied the centermost seats, from which they scrutinized the car like vultures. There was no way that Roger and MacInnes would be able to smoke cigars and drink whiskey without getting caught.

"Are you out of your mind?"

"Follow my lead," MacInnes whispered.

He fell into the aisle (overturning a game of checkers) and pretended to have a seizure. His legs jittered, his head pounded the floor, his mouth sprayed glittering foam. The boys closest to him recoiled in horror. Eventually, one of the masters rose with authority and seized command of the situation.

"Ah hem" were his exact words.

Roger's heart pounded. Stoney Batter would not be his first prep school. For reasons he didn't like to think about, he'd been quietly dismissed from two others. Following MacInnes would mean joining the wrong side of the law before he'd even arrived on campus. He would be a charlatan, a gangster, a hoodlum, a thief. It was the worst possible choice he could make.

Naturally, he sprang to his feet.

"My friend has the grippe," he announced, already dragging MacInnes by the armpits to the back of the train. "Should I take him outside for some air?"

Everyone looked at the man who'd taken charge: a master named Woodknight, who sported a heroic mustache that bristled with indecision. No doubt he was pondering three hours in a train that reeked of vomit—or worse.

"Right," Mr. Woodknight said. "See to that, will you?"

Roger opened the door and heaved MacInnes onto a roaring poop deck. He banged the door shut again. Through a grimy porthole, he watched Mr. Woodknight sit down.

They had actually pulled it off!

Roger and MacInnes dropped below the porthole and laughed like idiots above the roar of the wind and the clatter of train wheels. In unison, they loosened their neckties and unfastened their collars.

"I haven't had that much fun since yesterday," MacInnes said.

"I haven't had that much fun since ever!"

"You could've fooled me." MacInnes popped a cigar in Roger's mouth and struck a match on the safety rail. "The way you stood up to that bossy chap? You're a natural."

Roger puffed experimentally and hoped he didn't look like an amateur. He'd sneaked a few cigarettes in his time, but a cigar was something new. The smoke tasted horrible, and his eyes filled with tears. Waves of dizziness surged through his brain. It was a struggle just to follow the conversation.

"It was you who fooled me," he told MacInnes.

"How's that?"

"Reading poetry back there."

"Reading—?"

"So everyone would think you were a schoolmarm."

MacInnes dropped his jaw. "Is that what you thought?"

"It sure was. What a performance!"

"Look here," MacInnes said. "If we're going to be chums, you'll need to understand something. Poetry's my life."

"Oh." Roger blushed. "Well—I didn't mean anything."

"Of course you did," MacInnes persisted. "But it's all right. Our whole generation has forgotten the true meaning of poetry."

"What true meaning? Isn't poetry about flowers and stuff?"

"Hardly. Do you know why Plato wanted all the poets banished from his ideal republic?"

Roger frowned. He'd never taken much interest in Plato. Euclid and Pythagoras, more like it.

"Poetry's dangerous," MacInnes said finally. "It threatens the order of things. It questions authority. It's enough to scare the hell out of you. At least, when it's done right it is."

"You've scared me already."

MacInnes smiled sheepishly. "Sorry—it's my Romantic nature. I'm going out for the *Review*, you know."

"The literary rag? They're an exclusive bunch, aren't they?"

"Very. It'll probably take a month before they make me editor in chief."

"A whole month?" Roger snorted. "Has anyone ever mentioned how cocky you are?"

"All the time. Don't you like it?"

"I haven't decided."

MacInnes produced his flask, and they took turns drinking. "How about you?" he said. "What's your great passion?"

"Science," Roger said. "Physics and all that. What I'd really like to do is build flying machines. Aeroplanes, dirigibles. Maybe even moon rockets."

"You're joking!" MacInnes said.

"Don't you think it's possible?"

"Oh, it's not that. I just never thought I'd be chums with a bloody scientist, that's all!"

As the train barreled on through haystack hamlets and cornstalk villages, Roger and MacInnes fell asleep. When Roger awoke, MacInnes was snoring beside him. They were still on the poop deck, and the train was resting quietly at the Stoney Batter station. Roger jumped up—and immediately wished he hadn't. His head throbbed, and his mouth tasted like shoe leather. He looked through the porthole. The car was empty. So was the platform. Mr. Woodknight and the others had forgotten them.

That did it, Roger thought. No more tobacco—and *definitely* no more whiskey.

"Wake up," he said. MacInnes grunted and smacked his lips. Roger kicked him. "Wake up, you lunatic! We're here!"

"Don't tell the bishop," MacInnes said cryptically. Then he shook off the stupor and sat bolt upright. "Where?"

"Stoney Batter, where else?"

"Oh." MacInnes shuffled his suit coat over his head and went back to sleep. Roger wanted to join him, but he figured one of them ought to be responsible. The important thing was getting off the train. The logical plan was to retrace their steps through the car. He tried the door handle. It was locked. He beat the porthole with his fist.

8

2

Poetry should surprise by a fine excess.
—JOHN KEATS

Five minutes later they were motoring along the brick-paved streets of Stoney Batter the village, Roger hunched over the wheel of the stolen Ford, MacInnes calling out directions from the machine-gun seat: "Left! No, right! Turn here! Look, do you see where that man is? Avoid that street entirely. And for cripes sake, watch out for that horse! Yes, that's it. We're definitely lost."

"I thought you knew where you were going."

"Whatever gave you that idea? Oh, wait. That building ahead looks very official."

"It's the train station, you idiot. We've come full circle."

"Remarkable! We're not lost at all."

Roger slowed down as they passed the station, figuring they could ask someone directions to the campus. He was surprised to discover a pandemonium on the station lawn, which they had somehow overlooked the first time around. Beneath a large banner that read "Welcome Stoney Batter

Students," a crowd of masters and boys were eating water-melon and ice-cream sundaes.

"I should've known," Roger muttered.

On the station stairs, an Episcopal priest (in full regalia) looked up as the Tin Lizzie inched by. In a matter of moments, the expression on the old man's face shaded from quiet recognition to dawning awareness to fierce, burning rage. He cried out something and waved his black-garbed arms in the air.

"Do you suppose," MacInnes said, "that's Father Whosit?"

"The Dean Reverend?"

"Exactly. The fellow who beats chaps like us."

"Not only do I suppose that's him," said Roger, opening the throttle and stomping pedals, "but I think we've stolen his car!"

"Quick—turn down that way!"

If there was one thing Roger had learned during their brief relationship, it was that MacInnes's mental compass was invariably wrong. He spun the wheel in the opposite direction—and there, at the top of a long street lined with hundred-year-old oaks, loomed the columns and towers of the Stoney Batter Academy. They'd nearly made it. In the rearview mirror, he saw that the Dean Reverend had gathered a posse.

The chase was on.

"Stop!" someone cried. "Come back here, you rotten thieves!"

"Some welcome," MacInnes scolded.

Roger popped his foot off the first-gear pedal. He ground his molars in determination. The flivver backfired, trembled, sighed, then sped onward. Their freedom was short-lived.

The Stoney Batter Creek lay between them and the campus, and the only way across was a rickety one-lane bridge. The Ford itself would have fit easily—if it hadn't been for a horse-drawn ice wagon directly in their path.

Roger bleated his horn. "Get out of the way, you fool!"

If the driver heard, he didn't let on. Hoof by hoof, spoke by spoke, he and his cargo approached the ancient bridge.

"We're done for," Roger said.

"You've got to try *something*!"

"Do you want me to build an airship and fly us across?"

"How long will it take?"

Roger started to pass. The draft horse whinnied. The car lost traction. Gravel crunched beneath the tires and flew behind them like shrapnel. Boys and masters dropped for cover. With a sickening roar, the car hit the bridge and spun to the other side. Roger braked and looked around.

He couldn't have planned it better. The horse and wagon completely blocked the bridge. No one could follow them now.

Unfortunately, all that jostling had left the wagon in a tricky spot. Its left rear wheel sank into the road's muddy shoulder, pitching the wagon out of kilter. The driver leapt out of his seat and tried to brace the wagon from behind.

No good. It kept sinking. Half a dozen boys rushed to help—but the wagon was too heavy. The horse broke free from its harness, the wagon rolled backward, and its cargo splashed into the water.

The result was terrifying.

Clouds of steam bubbled out of the creek. Ghostly tendrils filled the air, and the mob disappeared in the grayness.

"What've you done?" MacInnes cried.

"The wagon must've been hauling dry ice," Roger said as he snapped on the windshield wiper. "It makes fog when you put it in water. It's a carnival trick really."

"Carnival trick? I thought we'd died and gone to hell."

"We'd better go somewhere, that's for certain."

And so they motored away through the clouds.

Soon they were driving past wide green lawns and an architectural mishmash of Victorian curlicues and sensible Georgian brick. Roger set the Ford's hand brake at Craxton House (it turned out they'd been assigned to the same dormitory) and they wrestled their stuff onto the portico.

"Too bad we didn't make it into Marshall House," Roger said.

"Oh?"

"Not that I'm a snob or anything."

"Course not."

"Just that Marshall is the *only* house on campus—if you want to go anywhere socially, that is. You know: sports, clubs—"

"Literary magazines?"

"That's what I've heard."

"Well, that's easy to fix. We'll just let everyone know that Michael MacInnes is here, and whatever house he lives in, that's the house to envy. It's very simple, once you think about it."

Impossibly, Roger believed him, believed every word. Somehow he knew that this madman poet had the power to make anything come true.

"What should we do with the car?" he asked.

"Get rid of it," MacInnes said. "Contraptions like that make me nervous."

Roger put the Ford in gear and sent it slowly up the road on its own. It cruised straight ahead for a few dozen yards, took a mischievous turn into the quadrangle, and was about to crash into a marble bench when it stopped of its own accord.

"Brilliant!" MacInnes said. "*Anyone* could've left it there."

As they stepped inside the Craxton House vestibule (looking for all the world like a couple of innocents) Roger felt a sudden pang of emptiness.

"Look here," he said to MacInnes. "I don't make chums easily, never have. And it's lousy to be the new kid in school. The other fellows all have their cliques, you know? What I'm trying to say is, after today—when the other fellows are here—do you think we'll still be chums, you and me?"

"Oh, sure." That winning smile. "Best of chums, I'd say."

3

But in her web she still delights
To weave the mirror's magic sights.

—ALFRED, LORD TENNYSON

MacInnes rang a bell by the ground-floor apartment. The hall where they waited stank of brass polish, floor wax, and chlorine bleach. Just like the orphanage. In a way it was a comfort. MacInnes hated to admit it, but coming to Stoney Batter was a little frightening. What if his schoolmates thought his poetry was too extreme? Worse: what if they didn't think of it at all?

He jangled the bell again.

"Be patient," Roger said. "I hear something."

Sure enough, the door cracked open, and an old man appeared. His chin was covered with white whiskers, and a porcelain teacup jiggled in a saucer in his hand. His flesh was marbled with veins and liver spots.

"Boys!" he exclaimed, bursting into a grin of corncob teeth. "Is the welcoming party over so soon?"

"We took a private car," MacInnes said.

"Really!" The old fellow studied them. "You're too old to

be freshmen," he said. "You must therefore be our entering juniors, Legrande and MacInnes. You're to be roommates, you know. I am Mr. Hamilton-Smythe, your house fellow. I am also your Latin master, so be forewarned. I expect your work to be done on time, and when you read aloud, I expect you to sound like Romans. Now—"

"Did he say we're going to be roommates?" Roger whispered.

MacInnes grinned. "Lucky break, eh?"

As Mr. Hamilton-Smythe embarked on a rambling discussion of Roman dialects, a breeze swung open the door to his apartment, exposing a room filled with books and dusty furniture. An old woman sat in what looked like a very uncomfortable chair. She wore a plain brown dress, and her hands were folded neatly in her lap.

"Hullo!" MacInnes called. "You must be Mrs. Hamilton-Smythe."

"How's that?" The old man whirled around. "Oh—yes." To the woman in the chair he said, "We have new boys, Elizabeth. What do you think? Do they look like keepers?"

The woman turned toward them, but her face was blank.

"She's been ill," Mr. Hamilton-Smythe said, and MacInnes knew it was an explanation he'd practiced.

"Perhaps," he said stupidly, "the new term will raise her spirits."

"Yes," Mr. Hamilton-Smythe said. "Perhaps it will."

It was an awkward moment, and MacInnes wished he could take it back and start over. How would it be, he wondered, to watch old age ruin someone you loved? How would it be to watch it happen to yourself? Better to die young, like

Byron or Shelley. Better just to sleep—perchance to dream. Anything but *this*.

Suddenly, Mr. Hamilton-Smythe was all business again.

"Daphne!" his phlegmy voice rattled down the hall. "Daphne!"

"Sir?" A boy in cockeyed spectacles was headed their way.

"These fellows are on your floor. Do me a favor and get them settled, eh? Show them around?"

"But, sir—I was just about to—"

"You can read your adventure stories later."

The boy glanced at an issue of *Argosy* magazine and tucked it inside his waist.

"Yes, sir," he grumbled. "Come along, you two."

They climbed two flights of marble stairs that wound through the building like the spine of some mythical beast.

"Your name isn't really Daphne," MacInnes said.

"It's what everyone calls me."

"What would you like us to call you?" Roger said.

"You're joking."

"Why do you say that?"

"I'm a sophomore. Sophomores don't get to choose anything."

"That's crazy," MacInnes said. "Why not?"

"I don't know. It's just the way things are."

As they rounded the first landing, MacInnes thought about the woman in the chair. What if she wasn't empty at all? What if her soul was only trapped inside, like a message in a bottle, waiting for someone to let it out?

"Tell me about Mrs. Hamilton-Smythe."

"Ooch," Daphne said. "She gives me the heebie-jeebies. What else do you want to know?"

"Does she ever say anything?"

"Not a word."

"And the old man takes care of her? How awful for him."

"Creepy's more like it."

Daphne led them to a room on the topmost floor.

"This is yours. Mine's next door. The lav is down the hall."

"Home at last!" MacInnes said hopefully. "Let's have a look."

The room was cramped, hardly more than a box, with drab wood furniture and iron bunks. A sagging window looked onto the ass end of Marshall House, where leaky rain gutters had painted the brickwork in shades of jaundice and bruise. This was where someone expected him to live? Ridiculous. Preposterous. Out of the question.

"Well?" MacInnes said to his roommate.

"Oh, no," Roger said, picking up the challenge. "This won't do at all. You'll have to show us another."

"Another *room*?" Daphne said. "This isn't a hotel, you know."

MacInnes went back to the hall and prowled from door to door. "All these other rooms are taken?" he asked.

"What do you think? Of course they are."

"How about this corner room? It looks half again as big."

"Not a chance," Daphne said. "That's Entwistle's room."

MacInnes and Roger shrugged. Who the devil was Entwistle?

"What about that one?" Roger said. "By the stairwell."

"You can't live in the storage room. It's off-limits."

"Show it to us anyway."

"But it's locked. Mr. H. has the only key."

"Daphne, Daphne, Daphne," MacInnes said. "If we're going to be chums, you'll have to give us more credit than that."

"Chums?" Daphne said. "I've never been chums before."

"You'll be chums with us then," Roger said.

MacInnes examined the door from several perspectives, held the knob, and adjusted it the way a jeweler might fine-tune a watch. The door popped open without a squeak.

"You don't spend your life in an orphanage without picking up a few things," he remarked.

Daphne frowned. "Entwistle isn't going to like this."

The door, it turned out, led to a hidden stairwell, which led to a fourth-story tower. MacInnes climbed to a musty chamber with windows on all four walls. The single room, twice as large as the one they'd been assigned, was packed with dirty mattresses, broken desks, and the abandoned memorabilia of countless former students, all of it layered with dust, webs, droppings, and mummified bugs. There was no electricity, but a half dozen gas jets poked through the walls. MacInnes tried one and was happy to discover it worked. Gaslight was infinitely more pleasing than electric. For heat, come winter, a filthy coal stove squatted in the corner.

"This is positively barbaric!" Roger said.

"Yes," MacInnes agreed. "Don't you love it?"

"We-ell. It certainly is big."

"Private, too. We don't have to worry about someone farting in the next room."

"I can set up my own laboratory."

"And I'll have space for all my books."

Roger opened a window. "Here's a nifty feature." He pointed to a widow's walk that cut across the roof beneath them. "A private balcony."

"What'd I tell you?" MacInnes grinned. "All right, Daphne. We'll take it."

Daphne stared at them. "You're both nuts," he said, "if you think Entwistle is going to stand for this."

"Now, look," MacInnes said. "I've had it up to here with this Entwistle fellow, and I haven't even laid eyes on him. Who is he?"

"Who's Entwistle? Well, this is his dormitory, isn't it?"

"I thought Hamilton-Smythe was in charge."

Daphne shook his head impatiently. "Mr. H. is only the house fellow. His word is law—but he's a master. He keeps his nose out of everyday business. That's Entwistle's headache. He's the house proctor. You at least know what that is, don't you?"

MacInnes did not.

"Holy cripes. The house proctor is a senior who's been given extra trust. It's his job to keep the roster, make sure we're in bed, lights out, no cooking, no women, no phonograph, no smoking, no liquor, no fun of any kind unless he says it's jake. Didn't you pay attention at the Dean Reverend's Welcome?"

"We skipped that nonsense," MacInnes told him.

"We had bigger fish to fry," Roger added.

"Like moving all this junk," MacInnes said, "before Entwistle comes along and tells us not to."

Daphne was incredulous. "Haven't you heard a thing I said?"

The next twenty minutes passed in a dusty blur of aching muscles, heaving lungs, slippery palms, toppling furniture, dented floorboards, and countless bags of rubbish tossed down the incinerator shaft. Roger showed off his engineering skills by switching locks and number plates with the room they were supposed to have taken. Now no one had to know the tower wasn't rightfully theirs.

"You guys won't last a week," Daphne predicted.

"Alas," MacInnes said. "The mind-forged manacles of man."

"Huh?"

MacInnes took the sophomore by his shoulders. "Fess up, Daphne. What're you so afraid of?"

"What do you mean?"

"Don't play coy with me, laddie. The Dean Reverend's Welcome hasn't finished yet. If you're so keen on going by the rules, why aren't you there?"

Daphne's eyes bulged until they filled the rims of his specs. "Hamilton-Smythe," he gasped. "He's coming!"

The boys leapt downstairs, slammed the tower door, and were sizing up the lavatory when Mr. Hamilton-Smythe came thumping down the hall, leaning on the handle of a blackthorn cane.

"Ah!" he said, puffing through his whiskers. "There you are, MacInnes. I was just reviewing your file, and I couldn't help noticing a letter from your old pastor. According to him, you have a real way with words. Poems, essays, that sort of thing. What about it?"

MacInnes shrugged. "I'm no Keats, if that's what you mean."

"Forget the modesty, man. Can you write or can't you?"

"I can."

"Splendid! I wonder if you've heard that every year Craxton and Marshall hold an Interhouse Competition. Craxton hasn't won in ages. We just don't have the talent. Not for the sporting events anyway. Marshall is stockpiled with athletes. Why, if it weren't for the Sykes boy, we'd have been positively *skunked* last year."

"I'm not sure I—"

"Hang on," Roger said. "Doesn't the competition finish with a rhetoric contest?"

Mr. Hamilton-Smythe nodded. "The Quintilian Oratory," he said with deep respect. "One boy from each house makes a ten-minute speech. It's worth a lot of points. It usually decides the whole competition."

"Oh!" MacInnes said. "You want *me* to speak for Craxton."

"It'd mean a lot to the house."

Pursing his lips thoughtfully: "I don't know if I'll have the time. You see, I'll be going out for the—"

"Tell you what. You agree to be the house speaker, and I'll pretend not to have noticed your, ah, housekeeping activities."

"Housekeeping?"

"I may be an old fossil, boys, but I haven't lost my wits."

Roger and Daphne turned red.

MacInnes just laughed. "Well, chums," he said. "It looks like he's got me!"

"You'll do it, then? Splendid! I'll speak to Entwistle about the room change and get back to you with the details."

The old man hobbled to the stairwell.

"And, boys?" he called over his shoulder. "Do me a favor and stay off the widow's walk, eh? It's falling apart—very dangerous. I don't know why we didn't have it torn down years ago."

4

My first thought was, he lied in every word.
—ROBERT BROWNING

After dinner (a mixture of macaroni and stewed tomatoes that some of the old boys called "dog brains") MacInnes took a walk around the campus. He couldn't help imagining that he'd been magically transported to Byron's Harrow or Shelley's Eton. He'd never seen so much grass, for one thing. The lawns seemed to roll on forever. Flower gardens lurked around every corner, and the air was alive with bees. Any moment now, a piping shepherd would drive his flock over the sidewalk. Cows would low, and satyrs would dance. If MacInnes couldn't find his muse here, he might as well give up.

On a whim, he followed a low stone wall until it disappeared into the woods. The campus was far behind him now, and the woods were thick. He spotted the remains of a footpath and knew at once he had to take it.

A few minutes later, he came to a cottage. Its ancient walls were green with moss, and its chimney puffed gouts of smoke.

Who the devil lived out here?

He was trying to decide whether he should knock or leave when a woman appeared on the doorstep and spoke to him in a voice that was as thick as Caribbean molasses.

"Come in," is what she said. "I've been expecting you."

She was impressive, to say the least. Her hair was wrapped in an orange turban that made her seem eight feet tall. Her dress was a rich shade of blue, and her skin was the color of polished wood. Her neck was adorned with a heavy gold chain. MacInnes had never seen anyone like her—and yet her presence at Stoney Batter made a strange kind of sense.

"You're sure it's me you were expecting?"

"In your pocket is a crust of bread. Give it to me, please."

"How did you know—?"

"Don't be stupid, boy. I know because I know."

He gave her the bread.

"My name is Aubergine Dubois. Please come inside."

He followed her into the cottage. Compared to Miss Dubois's extravagant looks, the interior was surprisingly plain. The only amenities were a few sticks of rough-hewn furniture and a large black pot bubbling over the fire.

She led him to a table, and they sat. Between them was a pail of chicken bones. At least he hoped they were chicken bones. They looked alarmingly like human fingers.

"Are you some kind of fortune-teller?" he asked.

"Pah! You are thinking of gypsies and other thieves. *I* am a student of the eternal mysteries."

"A sorceress, then."

"If the word pleases you."

"Can you see into the future?"

"Yes and no. It is true, I possess a special sight. But the future is not like the past. I see only the way things might be, not the way they must be. Otherwise, my powers would be a curse."

He thought it over and decided she was right. Knowing the future *would* be a curse. But having a *general* idea—that wouldn't be so bad, would it? It might even be good.

"Now," she said, "close your eyes and arrange the bones on the table."

"Does it matter how I arrange them?"

"No. The pattern you choose is the pattern that tells. The spirits will guide you."

"The spirits?"

She frowned. "Are you an unbeliever?"

"I believe in *something*. I'm just not sure what it is."

He reached into the pail and plucked out a bone. It was hard and dry and bore no traces of its former owner. He put the bone on the table.

The others went quickly.

When he was done, he opened his eyes and looked at the cipher before him. If it made any sense at all, he couldn't see it.

Miss Dubois, on the other hand, shivered with excitement.

"You are a very creative young man," she declared. "You have a talent for something. Are you a painter? Or perhaps a musician?"

"I'm a poet. That is—"

"Ah! I can see it now. How foolish of me to have missed it."

"Where?" MacInnes scanned the table. "Where do you see it?"

"In the bones, of course!"

"Which bones?"

"Yes," she said solemnly.

"Yes what?"

"They are indeed *witch bones*."

"What I meant was—"

"Your poetry," she went on, "will bring you great notoriety in the weeks to come. Your name will be the talk of the school."

"I knew it!"

"There is more. But the picture is unclear."

"Tell me anyway."

"It could be dangerous to speculate."

"I'll take my chances. Just tell me what you see."

"I see you falling in love with a beautiful girl."

MacInnes laughed. "I don't know if you've noticed, but Stoney Batter is a boys' school."

"Do you doubt my words?"

"It isn't that—"

"Then listen well. You will fall in love, but your love will present a dilemma. You will have to make a difficult choice."

"What choice?"

"The bones do not say."

"They're a cantankerous bunch, aren't they?"

"Hush! You will offend the spirits."

"I apologize. Do you see anything else?"

"A great many things. But it might be better if you found out for yourself."

"Oh, I get it now. You expect me to pay you."

"Don't be ridiculous. My insights are not for sale."

"Why tell me anything, then?"

Miss Dubois smiled and walked to the fire. She still had the crust of bread. She held it over the pot, which was bubbling like mad. Steam crawled up her arm.

"A time will come when I see you again," she said. "Thank you for visiting, Michael MacInnes."

How did she know his name? He didn't think he'd mentioned it. He was about to ask when she dropped the bread into the loathsome stew, and there was an explosion of blinding light.

MacInnes opened his eyes and looked around. The cottage had vanished. He was sitting on the ground in the middle of a ruin. His trousers were wet with dew, as if he'd been seated there for quite a while. He jumped to his feet and went to the place where the fire had been. A pile of stones was all that remained of the chimney. He touched the ancient hearth. It was cold. No one had lived here for at least a hundred years.

And Miss Dubois was nowhere in sight.

When MacInnes returned to the Craxton House tower, he found Roger sitting up in his bunk.

"I say, old chum. I've been led to believe there are girls in the vicinity. Know anything about it?"

Roger seemed surprised. "Are you pulling my leg?"

"I never joke about girls."

"But you must know about the Hood School."

"What's that? Sounds like a nunnery."

"It's only the most exclusive girls' school in the country. It's about five miles down the road."

MacInnes dropped his jaw. "No one told me that!"

"Just as well. The girls are strictly off-limits. Until the Fall Cotillion, that is."

"You mean my sex life hinges on a silly dance?"

"It's not just a dance. It's the event of the season. A sort of debutante ball. Daphne was telling me about it earlier. He said Hood School girls aren't allowed to socialize with us until we've been properly introduced. So every year, Stoney Batter puts on a fancy drag with colored lights and an orchestra, and everyone gets dressed up."

"Craziest thing I ever heard of," MacInnes said. "I mean, why get dressed up just to pet with a girl?"

"That's what I'm telling you. These aren't just—"

He was cut off by a freakish bellowing that echoed throughout the dormitory: "LIGHTS OUT, GENTLEMEN!"

"Cripes!" Roger said. "What was that?"

"I suspect it was that Entwistle chap."

"No wonder Daphne's afraid of him."

"Well, we'll see about that."

MacInnes dimmed the gas jets. He didn't feel like sleeping yet, so he climbed into an open window and pulled a package of Fatimas from his pocket. According to the label, it contained "the most skillful blend in cigarette history." Sure. He struck a match on the windowsill and blew smoke into the night.

He thought about Miss Dubois. She and the cottage had seemed so real. And his bread was really gone. He'd checked his pockets a dozen times over. But he might just as easily have lost it.

It was a puzzle, all right.

He flicked his cigarette out the window and climbed into

his bunk. Through the darkness, he noticed Roger thrashing restlessly about.

"What's the matter, old chum?"

Roger grumbled something into his pillow.

"Uh-oh," MacInnes said. "It's me, isn't it? I'm too dull to be friends with."

"It's not you."

"What then?"

"It's this tower. We must have the hottest room on campus."

"Of course."

They lay quietly for a while. In the distance, an illegal phonograph warbled something about a girl in Carolina.

"Look here," Roger finally said. "Have you ever done anything that was so wrong—so patently horrible and wrong—that you could never talk about it—not even with your best friend?"

"I'm not sure," MacInnes said. "I've never been close enough to anyone to find out."

"Never? I don't believe it."

"It's true. Growing up in an orphanage isn't as glamorous as you might think. Chums don't last. Just when you start to trust someone—whacko, he gets adopted, or fostered out somewhere. I suppose that's why I read so damned much. Poetry never runs out on you."

"You trusted me on the train—right from the start. Why?"

"You looked so out of place. And you hadn't said a word, not even to the porter. I thought, Here's a fellow misfit if ever I saw one."

"Misfit!" Roger cried.

"Would you rather be part of the golden set? With their baggy trousers and brilliantined hairstyles?"

"God, no. I just didn't think it was so obvious."

"Only to me," MacInnes said. "I'm sure everyone else thought you were perfectly normal."

"I'm not, though," Roger said. "Not at all."

"How do you mean?"

"That's just it. I *want* to tell you. But I can't."

MacInnes thought it over and realized he was keeping a few secrets of his own.

"Don't, then," he said.

"And you won't be sore?"

"Why should I be? You'll tell me when you're ready."

"Thanks," Roger said. "Hey, you know something?"

"What's that?"

"I think this year's going to turn out just fine."

"Of course it will, chum." MacInnes laughed. "You're rooming with me, aren't you? What more could you want?"

5

Happy those early days, when I
Shin'd in my angel-infancy!

—HENRY VAUGHAN

Walpole House, a Victorian monstrosity of gingerbread shingles and colorful gewgaws, was home to Stoney Batter's many clubs and fraternal societies. To MacInnes, observing it in the cool light of morning, it looked like a giant wedding cake.

He went into the foyer.

According to a cardboard sign, the offices of *The Stoney Batter Review* occupied the entire third floor. The problem, he discovered, was that no single set of stairs actually went to the third floor. He found his way to the second and fourth floors all right. But the passage to the third floor eluded him. Eventually, he surrendered and went back outside. He climbed up to three on the fire escape.

"Hah. Now we're getting somewhere."

The central feature of the room he entered was an enormous machine: a nightmare of gears, wheels, and cryptic levers. It was grimy and smelled of ink. He tiptoed around it and walked quietly to the front of the building. Three upper-classmen were loafing on broken-down couches. They looked like decent enough fellows—a bit prissy, perhaps—but he figured he'd better get used to that. The thing that troubled him was that they wore identical green fedoras. Some sort of club uniform? He hoped not. Hats made his scalp itch.

"So, how are things coming with that girl of yours, Trent?" he overheard one of the chaps saying. "You get anything over the summer?"

"Yeah, Romeo," said another. "Give us the scoop."

"It so happens," the third chap said carefully, "that Miss Waverly and I have a genuine respect for each other."

"What you mean is, she's still putting the freeze on you."

"Utterly."

"That's a shame."

"A real waste of talent."

"Especially when there're so many girls who don't mind it."

"And a few who even like it."

"That's right, Trent. You ought to tell her about that."

"Believe me, I've told her. It makes no difference. She's got a will of her own."

"So, what're you going to do?"

"To put it bluntly, I may have to *force* the issue."

"You mean . . ."

"Gosh."

"Are you sure about that, Trent?"

"Don't you think I'm entitled?"

"Well, yeah . . ."

"It just sounds a bit extreme."

"Not at all. In fact, I'll be doing her a favor. A girl like Laura needs the man to be assertive. You see that, don't you?"

"I suppose."

"There's no supposing about it, Biff. I've paid my dues, and I have a right to expect certain things in return."

MacInnes wondered what to do. Now was definitely a poor time to make himself known. But if he put it off any longer, they might think he'd been listening on purpose.

He cleared his throat, and the three chaps looked up.

"Cripes!" said the one called Biff. "Scare me half to death!"

"I say . . ." Romeo eyed MacInnes suspiciously. "What's your game, friend? Don't you know it's discourteous to eavesdrop on private conversations?"

"Er—sorry," MacInnes said. "I couldn't find the stairs, so I came in the back."

"Through the window?"

"There's a fire escape."

"There is?"

"I just climbed it."

"Well," Romeo blustered, "next time come in properly."

MacInnes looked around. "Is this the *Review* office?"

"I certainly hope so."

"And you're the editor in chief?"

"I am indeed. Trent Bloxom's the name. And you are—?"

"Michael MacInnes. I want to join up."

"I don't think I've met you." Bloxom sniffed. "You don't live in Marshall House, do you?"

"Craxton."

"And what makes you think we need a Craxton House boy?"

"What makes you think you don't?"

"Well, the filth on your trousers, for one thing. You look as if you fell off an oyster boat."

MacInnes glanced at his clothes and shrugged. After the last few days, he'd been sure they looked much worse.

"They'll launder out," he said. "What's the big fuss?"

"The *Review* has a reputation to uphold. We don't take on just anybody, you know. And we certainly don't take on vagabonds. Come back during Rush Week with the rest of the freshmen, and we'll see how you measure up."

"Freshmen!" MacInnes said. "I happen to be a junior, thanks all the same. And as far as that reputation stuff goes, I'm not the one who's plotting to 'force the issue' with his girlfriend."

"Well, I hardly see—"

"What's more, you'll be damned lucky to have me."

Bloxom sighed. "I suppose you have experience?"

"Gosh, yes."

"On the magazine at your old school, were you?"

"Well." MacInnes frowned. "We didn't exactly have one."

"The newspaper, then?"

MacInnes shook his head.

"I don't suppose your father edits *The Saturday Evening Post*?"

"No."

"Then what sort of experience *do* you have?"

"I write," he said simply.

Bloxom fixed him with a look of penetrating boredom. "Don't tell me. You're a poet."

"The most noble occupation—though I confess I have composed a meditation or two."

"Look here, MacArthur—"

"That's MacInnes. M-A-C, capital I—"

"The fact is, we have enough poets on staff already."

"Not like me, you don't."

"Some sort of literary genius, are you?"

"That's it." He looked around the room. "Do you think I might have a desk near the window? Fresh air inspires me."

"Let's decide if we even want you before we offer you a desk, eh? What sort of poetry do you write?"

Finally, a question MacInnes could answer intelligently.

"It's like Whitman," he said. "Or Blake. You know—religious satire, philosophical speculation about man's place in the cosmos, that sort of thing. I used to write sonnets, but I think the form is exhausted by now, don't you?"

"Exhausted!"

"Well, it's a neat trick and all—cramming your thoughts into fourteen lines. But it's a bit forced, don't you think? I mean, even the best poet has to wonder if he's used a word because it's really the *best* word, or if it's just the best word that fits the rhyme, do you see?"

Bloxom nodded. "Oh, I see, all right—I see you've been taken in by a bunch of Modernist hogwash."

"I have?"

"Gawd, yes. Don't you realize most of the poetry that's been written over the last thirty years has been part of an anarchist conspiracy?"

MacInnes had never heard anything so deranged in his life. "An anarchist *what?*"

"You heard me," Bloxom said. "No respect for rhyme and meter. No respect for tradition. I tell you, it's up to people like me to keep literature from going to the dogs."

By now, MacInnes wanted to hit him. What he said was "That's an interesting point of view. Just out of curiosity, what sort of poetry do *you* like?"

The question seemed to flatter Bloxom—he almost smiled.

"Well, there's Shakespeare, of course. But Milton is my first love. Without a doubt, *Paradise Lost* is the greatest—"

"How do you feel about Byron?" MacInnes said.

"An incestuous pornographer."

"Shelley?"

"An atheist."

"Keats?"

"Oh, his *ideas* are intriguing."

"But?"

"Too many nouns."

"You're joking."

"Look here, MacDonald—"

"MacInnes. The G is silent."

"—I'm sure you're a talented writer in your own unique way, but it's obvious—"

"Hang on, there, Trent."

Biff gestured for the editor to join him by the big machine. They whispered for a moment, then Bloxom clapped his chum on the shoulder.

"I say—that's a dandy idea! Come over here, ah . . ."

MacInnes joined them. Standing eye to eye with the editor, he was startled to find that Bloxom had at least three inches on him. No doubt his height contributed to his arrogance.

"Do you know what this is?" Bloxom said.

MacInnes eyed it skeptically. "Something left over from the Inquisition?" he guessed.

"Eh? No, no. It's a Chandler and Price Gordon letter-press."

"Is that supposed to mean something?"

"It's supposed to print the magazine. But look at the shape it's in!"

"Oh?"

"A press like this needs to be thoroughly cleaned after every job. Does *this* look clean?"

MacInnes had to admit it did not. The gears were plugged with oil and paper pulp. The type was clogged with ink. He doubted the apparatus could even work in this condition.

"Last year's staff never once bothered to clean it. And it's been coagulating all summer long."

"It is pretty dreadful," MacInnes said.

But Bloxom was eyeing him kind of funny. "We'll take you on," the editor said, "if you agree to clean the press."

MacInnes waited for the laugh. It never came.

"But it's impossible!" he protested. "You can't be serious?"

"You'll find everything you need in the cellar."

"But—!" MacInnes took a deep breath. This might be his only chance. "Let's say I do clean it. *Then* do I get to write?"

"Eventually, I suppose. There's more to publishing a magazine than writing, you know."

"Like what?"

"We desperately need someone to sell advertising space."

MacInnes felt sick. "I'm a poet, not a huckster! Let me write some content. Let me give the magazine some vision."

"That's my job," Bloxom snapped. "I can't just turn it over to a new boy. Most fellows come on when they're freshmen and *work* their way to the top."

"I'm not most fellows."

"Take it or leave it."

MacInnes thought it over. A chance to work on the *Review* was half the reason he'd come to Stoney Batter. He wouldn't even mind cleaning the press. William Blake was a printer, and if *he* didn't mind the muck, why should MacInnes? But with an overstuffed bully like Bloxom in charge, he knew he'd never publish a line.

"Will I have to wear one of those hats?" he said finally.

"Of course," Bloxom said. "It's a *Review* tradition."

"I was afraid you'd say that."

"You—?"

"Green's just not my color."

Bloxom was dumbfounded. "You mean *you're* turning *us* down?"

"I'm afraid so."

"Because of the *hat?*"

Biff interrupted them again. "Come off it, Trent. He's pulling your leg."

"Aw, don't tell him that," MacInnes said. "Another minute and he'd've begged me to sign on."

"Pulling my leg?" Bloxom echoed. "Get out of here—and don't bother coming back. You'll never work for the *Review,* understand? Not this year, not next. I'll make sure of it."

"That suits me fine," MacInnes said. "Bunch of snotty prigs."

In a minute he was clanking back down the fire escape. He didn't belong here, and he'd been a fool to think otherwise.

But if he didn't belong on the *Review,* where did he belong?

So much for Miss Dubois's prophecy.

6

On what wings dare he aspire?
What the hand dare seize the fire?

—WILLIAM BLAKE

Something slimy was stirring in the pit of Howard Entwistle's gut. He did not like change. He loathed disorder. He abhorred surprise. He especially hated new boys. And the two new boys who had usurped the tower were threatening the stability of the house. Something would have to be done—now—before classes began and the semester spun out of control.

"Edgar," he snapped. "What's taking so long?"

"That was the last stitch, Howard."

Edgar Sykes was Entwistle's muscular roommate. He pulled a length of thread to his teeth and bit off the excess, then smoothed out the wrinkles he'd left in the trousers of Entwistle's seersucker suit. This magnificent garment of blue and white stripes (tailor-made by Sterling & Wick) seemed to have shrunk over the summer. It was irritating. Or might have been. Among his many talents, Edgar was proficient with the needle—oh, yes, proficient indeed. Entwistle stepped into the crackling folds of cool cotton cloth, buttoned his fly, and let out his breath.

The trousers fitted him perfectly.

"My bucks!" he said to Edgar. "Hurry!"

Entwistle shifted his massive rump into a cordovan chair and let Edgar fasten a pair of white buckskin shoes to his feet. Then he rose—with some difficulty—and admired himself in the mirror.

"Good show, Edgar!" he exclaimed. "You've really done it!"

"Aw, shucks, Howard. You know I like doing stuff for you."

"I say this calls for a treat."

Edgar frowned. "What treat?"

"Some chocolate, of course."

"Oh! Swell idea, Howard."

Entwistle tore open a Hershey's bar and crammed it into his mouth. The bittersweet confection exploded on his tongue, foamed between his teeth, and flowed down his throat. He opened another and was about to repeat the performance when he remembered poor Edgar. He broke off a morsel, gave it to his friend, and devoured the rest in one bite.

Exhausted, he fell back into his cordovan chair and watched Edgar do calisthenic exercises in the corner.

At a hundred and sixty pounds of muscle and sinew, Edgar was the athletic champion of Craxton House. He played a varsity sport in every season—football, wrestling, track and field—and was widely considered the strongest man on campus.

Entwistle, on the other hand, detested sports. His physique was an example of nature's cruelty. His heart was weak.

His bowels were enigmatic. And the pimples on his face—well, never mind. The steady rhythm of Edgar's contortions made him drowsy. Soon, he fell into the old despair, and the outlaws in the tower drifted to the shadows of his mind.

He sighed. "I should have more restraint."

"The chocolate?"

"The chocolate."

"But you lost so much weight over the summer."

"You're only saying that."

"Are you kidding? It's obvious."

"That's what I wanted to believe," Entwistle said. "But all my clothes are so tight. I thought—that is, I feared . . ."

"They've shrunk, is all. It's the humidity that does it."

"You could be right," Entwistle allowed. "The humidity."

"Of course I'm right." Edgar rubbed some oil on his muscles. "You know what you should do?"

"Tell me."

"You should march right up to those new boys and tell 'em how things work around here. Make sure they know who's boss."

Entwistle shook his head. "I can't. What if they laugh at me?"

"They won't laugh at you. You're a proctor, a man of importance. They'll see that."

"They won't." Entwistle sobbed. "It'll be like freshman year all over again."

His memory flashed to a night when he'd been dragged from the bath, all naked and slippery, then wrapped in a blanket and beaten by a gang of thugs. *Take that, fatty!* his anonymous housemates had said. *Take that!* Most of those fellows had graduated by now, but it made no difference. The memory haunted him all the same. His skin grew clammy, his heart pounded in his chest. It was too fast, he thought. The doctor had said—

"And of course there's business," Edgar added.

"Business?"

"Throckmorton's at Yale now. The market belongs to you."

"Yes." Entwistle took a deep breath. "Yes, it does."

"Think of all the money we'll make."

"Yes." His heart slowed to a gentle throb. "The money."

"No one will laugh at you then, Howard."

"Not even the new boys?"

"The new boys will respect you."

"Yes." Entwistle nodded. "Yes, they will."

The change was nothing short of miraculous. One minute he was the butt of a thousand humiliations. The next he was a senior, a proctor, a man with power and destiny. Warmth flowed through his veins. He was healed.

"Thank you, Edgar," he said. "Sometimes I forget who I am."

Entwistle knocked on the tower door. His only answer was silence. He knocked again. This time he heard a rustle of paper. He tried the knob, and the door opened onto the fragrance of Eastern fantasy: cinnamon, coriander, ginseng, orange peel. The old stairs creaked as he climbed through layers of blue smoke.

At the top, he found himself in a bohemian psychosis.

Busts of Keats and Byron frowned at him from packing-crate bookshelves. Hindu nymphs flaunted their breasts on tapestries hung from the ceiling. Incense and candles smoldered on every available surface. In the center of the room, sitting like Buddha on a large batik pillow, was a fellow with unruly hair. He was scribbling furiously in a notebook. He was also quite naked.

"Legrande?"

No answer.

"MacInnes?"

The fellow stopped writing and spoke in a world-weary voice: "I would to Heaven that I were so much clay."

"Uh—" Entwistle was startled. "You *are* Michael MacInnes?"

"You got it."

"What the devil are you up to?"

"I am writing a modern epic. I call it *Paradise Abandoned*."

"Nice title. My name is Howard Entwistle. I'm—"

"—the house proctor. I've been expecting you."

"You have?"

"Administrative stooges always find me eventually."

Entwistle's teeth clicked. "I am not a stooge."

"That's what they all say."

Entwistle strode indignantly about the room. He did not like MacInnes—he'd known it the instant he'd laid eyes on the peculiar décor—and he was frustrated that his usual tactics were having so little effect.

"You realize," he said, "that I already have enough evidence to get you beaten. Incense and candles pose a fire hazard. That's why they're forbidden. And do I smell *tobacco*?"

"My last cigarette." MacInnes yawned. "I'm reforming."

"Is that a fact? It seems to me I could search this room and find enough contraband to have you thrown out of school."

"You won't do it, though."

"What makes you so certain?"

"You want something from me."

Entwistle shrugged. He took a bottle of whiskey from his hip pocket and held it up as an offering. MacInnes dressed himself in trousers and a sweater and fetched a pair of glasses. Entwistle poured, but MacInnes seemed reluctant to drink.

"Do I surprise you?" Entwistle asked.

"I'm not sure yet."

"I have a complicated personality."

"Uh-huh."

"As the philosopher says, there are no such things as moral deeds. There are only moral interpretations of deeds."

"Nietzsche." MacInnes shook his head. "I might have guessed."

"So I've impressed you!"

"You make a strong impression."

"Well put. Let us drink to a lasting friendship."

MacInnes toyed with his glass. "There's no hurry."

"We'll talk then."

"Oh?"

"We're rebels, you and I. Revolutionaries. Leaders of men."

"You're afraid of me."

Entwistle blushed. This was not going well.

"Afraid?" he said. "Quite the contrary. I simply want you to understand that there can be only one man in charge of the house. If you fight me, I can make your life miserable. If you help me, I can make both our lives better."

"I doubt it."

"You'd be surprised. There's a *fortune* to be made here."

"Bootlegging whiskey?"

"My most popular item. Try some, please."

MacInnes seemed to make a decision. He took a sip, swished it around his mouth, and spit it back into his glass.

"Aargh!" he said. "What're you trying to do, kill me?"

"What do you mean?"

"This stuff is poison!"

"You're lying," Entwistle stammered. "This stuff is the real McCoy. I—I have it brought down from Canada by boat."

"In a pig's eye. Somebody made that stuff in a shack, and he did a lousy job. Drink enough, you'll go blind—if it doesn't rot your liver first. Why do you think they call it 'coffin varnish'?"

"I suppose you're an authority on the subject."

"I know enough."

Entwistle breathed deeply and tried not to panic. "So what if it's not real?" he said. "It's a good imitation. Good enough for a bunch of kids."

"That story won't play when somebody croaks."

"Nobody's going to croak! I've been selling this stuff for over a *year*."

"You've been lucky, that's all."

Entwistle thought for a moment. "Perhaps I am," he said. "Perhaps we're both lucky. A fellow like you probably has connections, eh?"

"A few. Back in the—" MacInnes paused. "Back in the city."

"Say you wanted a case of the real stuff. Could you get it?"

"Probably."

"Anything you wanted? Whiskey—gin—brandy?"

"Sure."

"See that? I knew you were the man I wanted to talk to. With your connections—and my distribution system—we could clean up."

"Sorry," MacInnes said.

"I beg your pardon?"

"Look, I'm no angel. But I don't hurt anybody if I can help it, and I don't like people who do. So take your partnership—*and* your tarantula juice—and get the hell out of my tower."

Stomach acid flooded the back of Entwistle's throat. "You're making a mistake," he said.

"Buster, I've been making 'em all day."

"Don't expect me to repeat the offer."

"Don't expect me to change my mind."

Entwistle stood and retrieved his bottle. He thrust his hands into his pockets to disguise their shaking, turned his back on MacInnes, and shambled down the stairs.

"Hey!" MacInnes called after him. "You keep that poison away from my chums, you hear?"

Edgar Sykes opened a small leather case. He removed an ampule of morphine and a glass syringe. He swabbed the needle with peroxide and filled the syringe with life-restoring medicine.

"Hurry, Edgar! Hurry!"

"Are you *sure* you want me to do this?"

"That bastard showed me no respect at all."

"Aw, Howard—"

"Look at me! I'm sweating. My bowels are in a knot. My entire body itches—"

"Aw, Howard—"

"Damn you, Edgar, do I have to do it myself?"

"No." Edgar sighed. "I'll do it."

The swab was cold on Entwistle's arm. The needle pricked his skin. An icy warmth flowed straight to his heart, and crystals of darkness fell over his eyes. One last moment of clarity before the dream-mother pressed him to her bosom: MacInnes would have to be dealt with.

7

I became myself capable of bestowing animation upon lifeless matter.

—MARY WOLLSTONECRAFT SHELLEY

Roger gaped at the shiny black counters, the glittering glassware, the dull brown bottles of chemical reagents, the stoppered green jugs of biological specimens. He peeped through a microscope, ran his fingers across a triple-beam balance. In a well-equipped lab, he thought, you could shine the light of reason on nature's most enduring secrets. How vast was the universe? What was the tiniest speck of matter? Why did most boys like girls—while some, a very few, did not?

He was startled by a noise at the back of the room.

His first thought was to leave—he probably wasn't allowed here before classes started—but curiosity drove him forward. The noise, it turned out, had been made by Mr. Woodknight. The master was conducting an experiment.

Roger watched in silent fascination.

With one hand, Mr. Woodknight held a struggling frog against a counter. With the other, he punched a hatpin through the frog's skull and jiggled it all around. The technique was called pithing: destroy the brain without injuring the body. Grisly to the layman, but Roger knew it was painless. The frog soon lay dead.

Now the serious work could begin.

Mr. Woodknight made an incision along the frog's spine. With practiced fingers, he peeled back the flesh. Then he stimulated the exposed nerves, one at a time, with the tip of an electrified probe.

At first, nothing happened.

Then, slowly, a foot began to twitch.

Then one of the legs began to tremble.

Finally, the cadaver itself hopped into the air and landed *splat* on the floor.

"Fantastic!" Roger blurted.

Mr. Woodknight must have known he had an audience. He wasn't the least bit startled. He picked up the frog and put it back on the counter.

"Like to give it a try?" he said.

"Are you sure?"

"Be my guest."

Roger took the probe from Mr. Woodknight's hand and mimicked the procedure. Sure enough, the frog hopped—though not quite as energetically as before.

"Are you interested in biology?" Mr. Woodknight asked.

"I'm interested in all the sciences."

"Do you understand what we've been doing?"

"I think so. Nerves interact electrochemically. Stimulating a nerve with electricity shortcuts the process. I've read about it, but I've never seen it done before."

"It makes an impressive demonstration. I'm just getting ready for tomorrow's freshmen."

"Is it useful?"

"I can count on at least three boys fainting every year."

"I mean, does the process have any practical applications?"

Mr. Woodknight fingered his mustache. "Not really. Not yet anyway. But the century's hardly begun. Who knows what some plucky inventor will think of?"

He frowned a bit. "Do I know you?"

Roger panicked. "I don't think so."

"Are you sure I didn't see you on the train yesterday?"

"I took a private car."

"Oh, yes, I see."

Roger ran all the way to the tower.

"MacInnes!" he cried. "You won't believe it!"

MacInnes was lying in the center of the floor, surrounded by scraps of paper. He'd been writing.

"Has the world come to an end?" he said hopefully.

"What? No . . ."

Roger described his experience in the lab. MacInnes listened politely but failed to share his enthusiasm.

"It's ghoulish," he pronounced.

"It's science."

"It's appalling. Haven't you ever read *Frankenstein*?"

"Yes—and as I recall, the protagonist was a lot like you: headstrong, romantic—"

"Insane?"

Roger hurled himself into his bunk. "What's got you in such a mood?" he said. "Weren't you going to dazzle those fellows at the *Review* today?"

It was exactly the wrong question to ask.

"Those bastards," MacInnes said. "I told 'em to piss off."

"You didn't!"

"I most certainly did—the instant I realized they wanted nothing to do with me."

"Gosh, I'm sorry."

"Don't be, old chum. I'm better off without 'em."

"Then you're not disappointed?"

"Of course I'm disappointed. What's a poet without readers?"

"Oh."

"The only thing that bothers me is, they never even gave my work a chance. This editor chap, Bloxom, didn't like my trousers or something, and that was the end."

"So why not start your own magazine?"

"Just like that?"

"You know where the equipment is. How hard could it be?"

MacInnes brooded.

"I'd have to break into the office after curfew," he said.

"I suppose you would."

"And someone would have to help me run the press."

"No doubt."

"It'd be dangerous. The sort of thing one gets expelled for."

"Exactly."

"Would you—?"

Roger laughed. "After what we've been through already? I wouldn't miss it for the world."

8

I believe in the flesh and the appetites . . .
—WALT WHITMAN

The next morning, MacInnes awoke with the sun and climbed out to the widow's walk for a cigar. The wooden parts were gray, and the entire structure was as run-down as Mr. Hamilton-Smythe had said. He threw his weight against a handrail as a sort of test, and the rail popped loose. He nearly plunged into the quad. He puffed his cigar and wondered how long it would have taken to hit the ground. Two seconds? Three? And in the last possible moment, would the Almighty have plucked his soul from his body and spared him the pain of death? He doubted it very much.

"Hey, MacInnes!" Roger called from the window. "Quit fooling around or we'll be late."

He climbed back inside the tower.

When the orphanage had arranged for MacInnes's scholarship, they'd given him a stipend. He'd spent most of the money on clothes: gray flannel trousers, white shirt and collar, school-striped tie, and a brass-buttoned blazer with the Stoney Batter seal embroidered over the breast pocket.

He showered, shaved, and put on this ridiculous costume.

"What do you think?" he asked Roger.

"Who are you, and what have you done with Michael MacInnes?"

"I knew it."

Roger laughed. "I was kidding. You look very nice."

"I look like something mass-produced in a factory."

"Better get used to it."

"Fie! Conspirator! *Et tu*, Legrande?"

At breakfast, he settled for a bowl of oatmeal and a slice of fatty ham.

A bell rang, and he was off to classes. Mr. Hamilton-Smythe was impressed with his vocabulary, so he knew Latin would go all right. History was another matter. It was all he could do not to pull out his hair when Edgar Sykes remarked how crazy it had been for Cortés and his soldiers to burn their boots. "Think of the splinters they must have gotten in their feet." ("Boats!" MacInnes wanted to cry. "They burned their bloody boats! Do you think they *walked* across the ocean?")

During a break, he found a closet and sneaked a few desperate puffs of tobacco. He remembered what Roger had said about the Dean Reverend's paddle and knew he'd eventually have to give up the habit. He just didn't want to. When time was up, he pinched the coal between his fingers and stashed the unfinished cigar in his pocket. With luck, he wouldn't set himself on fire.

Lunch was a bowl of lima beans flavored with fatty ham.

MacInnes's first afternoon class was Religion, taught by the Dean Reverend himself. By now MacInnes had learned that the Reverend Hezekiel Grimstaff was not only the school's chief disciplinarian but also its headmaster and spiritual adviser. He never smiled, never laughed, and never wore less than a complete set of vestments, even when he was teaching. He was unmarried, abstained from liquor and tobacco, and, it was rumored, brushed his teeth with Fels Naptha soap. He was such a model of piety, in fact, that when he walked into the classroom, with a Bible in one hand and a box of chalk in the other, MacInnes almost fell to his knees and begged forgiveness. For what, he wasn't sure.

The Dean Reverend's first lecture was a doozy.

"In recent years," he began, "it has become fashionable to believe that Man is descended from apes, that the universe is millions of years old, and that God had no part in its creation. Rest assured, all of this is nonsense."

MacInnes looked at his classmates, all hastily writing notes as if the Dean Reverend's opinion were infallible.

Sheep.

"I want you to consider an analogy," the old fellow went on. "If a man were walking through the mountains and he came upon a pebble, he would surely be right in believing that the pebble had lain there since time out of mind, without giving much thought to why it was there or what function it was meant to serve. Doesn't that make sense?"

A murmured assent was barely audible above the scratching of pens.

"Now imagine that our man came upon a pocket watch half-buried in the soil. Imagine that he opened the watch and noticed the works, saw the gears moving in perfect coordination, and the hands moving in time to the gears. Surely he would be right in believing that the watch had not come into being by some accident—that it had been designed by some intelligence—and that its parts moved as they did for some purpose. Doesn't that also make sense?"

Again the murmured assent.

"So it is with the world," the Dean Reverend concluded. "Is it an accident that the earth is perfectly suited to man's needs? When he thirsts, he finds water. When he hungers, he finds beasts and vegetables. When he is cold, he finds wool. The list goes on. My point is this. When it is so obvious that the entire world has been designed for the good of man, how could anyone deny that the designer must be God?"

There were a few moments of silence, and then the boys began to clap. All but MacInnes, that is.

"May I ask a question?" he said.

The Dean Reverend squinted at him. "You're—?"

"MacInnes, sir."

"Ah, yes. One of our new boys."

MacInnes swallowed and wondered if he was about to make a terrible mistake.

"In your first analogy," he said, "the man could tell the difference between a pebble and a pocket watch by seeing that the watch had a purpose and the pebble had none. Is that correct, sir?"

"Quite so, quite so."

"And in the second part, you said that simply observing the world reveals that it too must have been designed with a purpose."

"Yes—?"

"I suppose I'm just confused. In the first case, you claimed that the natural world—in the form of a pebble—has no purpose. In the second case, you claimed that the natural world does have a purpose. It just seems like a contradiction, that's all."

The Dean Reverend chewed at his bottom lip.

"They were two different arguments," he said finally. "Now—"

"Yes, sir." MacInnes pressed on. "I just thought they should be logically consistent, that's all."

"But they are consistent."

"They are?"

"Certainly! They're consistent with the word of God. That's the only consistency you should worry about."

"But—" He wanted to point out that the Dean Reverend was guilty of circular reasoning: using his conclusion to justify the evidence that was supposed to support his conclusion. He never got the chance.

"Thank you, MacInnes. Don't you think it's time we gave some other boys a chance to be heard?"

The Dean Reverend raised his eyebrows and shot a warning look to the rest of the class. If MacInnes did have any allies, they wouldn't be speaking up now.

"No one?" the Dean Reverend said. "Let's move on, then. Open your Bibles to the Book of Genesis . . ."

His last class of the day was Advanced Literature, taught by a Mr. Moffett, whom MacInnes instantly admired for his rumpled tweeds and gravy-stained tie. Unfortunately, the class was also attended by the insufferable Trent Bloxom. To say the least, it would be an interesting semester.

"Welcome to Advanced Literature," Mr. Moffett said. "Each of you is here because you managed to convince someone you were ready for the class. Personally, I have my doubts—so I have prepared a test of your literary knowledge. No, no, leave your pens in their boxes. This will be an oral examination."

Mr. Moffett glanced at a roster and picked out a slender boy.

"Mr. Atkinson," he said. "Who wrote 'How do I love thee? Let me count the ways'?"

"That's an easy one, sir. Mrs. Browning did."

"Very good." Mr. Moffett smiled. "Mr. Bloxom, please identify the form of Mrs. Browning's poem."

"It's an Italian sonnet, sir. That means—"

"Yes, I know what it means. We'll get to that later."

Bloxom scowled. Mr. Moffett consulted his roster again.

"Mr. Cartwright, this ought to be simple. Is it a good poem?"

" 'How Do I Love Thee'?"

"Stay with us, Mr. Cartwright."

"Well—yes, sir. Of course it's a good poem."

"What makes you certain?"

"Well—we studied it last year with Mr. Kleindorf."

"What's that got to do with anything?"

"Well—Mr. Kleindorf wouldn't have us studying nonsense, would he?"

"That's the question I'm putting to you."

"Oh. Well—I'm not sure. I mean—I assumed it was good."

"But is it? Mr. Hawkens? Mr. Koch?"

Mr. Moffett threw his roster across the room and sighed. "Look, I'm sure you're all very good with names and dates and iambic pentameter—but have you ever once thought about quality?"

MacInnes noticed that Bloxom was wetting his lips, prefatory to speaking, and for some reason it seemed important to stop him. MacInnes raised his hand quickly and said: "It's an *adequate* poem."

"Adequate?" Mr. Moffett looked at MacInnes now. "Your name is . . . ?"

"MacInnes, sir."

"Please clarify your answer, Mr. MacInnes."

"I mean, it looks like a sonnet, and acts like a sonnet, and I'm sure it's very appealing to the sort of girl who simply wilts at the mention of love. But it doesn't say very much, and what it does say is not what I'd call sincere."

"Go on."

"Well, it's obvious, isn't it? All that 'depth and breadth' business. That's not *love*—not real love anyway. It's more like directions for planting lettuce."

Mr. Moffett laughed, and most of the students joined him.

"A solid answer, Mr. MacInnes. Debatable—but solid. Now, as the reigning expert, can you give us an example of a *sincere* love poem?"

MacInnes thought it over.

"Do hurry." Bloxom yawned. "We're all desperate to hear a Craxton boy's opinion."

MacInnes took a chance and recited a quatrain from memory:

I have tasted the apple, and suckled the fruit,
And chewed the raw grain, and drunk the rose hips.
Yet still none compare, not the corn, nor the root,
To the sweet, dawning dew of your lips.

The class was silent. Even Mr. Moffett seemed taken aback.

"I'll be damned," he said. "I've flunked my own test. Who is it? No, wait—let me guess. All that fruit reminds me of Campion. But the earthiness of the grain and the roots—it must be later. Romantic, I believe. It's too sensual for Wordsworth, however. More likely Keats. Except that I wrote my thesis on Keats, and I have never encountered this poem."

Mr. Moffett smiled, obviously pleased. "I give up," he said. "Who is it?"

"No one you'd know," MacInnes said. "A very minor poet."

"Romantic?"

"Modern."

"I'll be damned. What's his name? I assume it's a he?"

"Yes, sir. His name is . . . Michael MacInnes."

"You mean you wrote it yourself?"

"Yes, sir. A few years ago. Back in my rhyming period."

"Well, congratulations. I think you've really got something."

"Thank you, sir."

Mr. Moffett looked over at Bloxom. "You hear that, Trent? Some new talent for the *Review*."

"Imagine that," Bloxom said bitterly, as if the words were poison in his mouth. "How lucky for us all."

9

And from his blazon'd baldric slung
A mighty silver bugle hung.

—ALFRED, LORD TENNYSON

Daphne sat in Mr. Hamilton-Smythe's classroom, silently
mouthing passive verb conjugations. It was torture. Not
because he hated Latin (though he did wonder why they
should be forced to study a dead language). But because *every*
class was torture. The chorus of whispers never let up—the
same old voices, the same old taunts. Had there really been a
summer, or was it only something he'd dreamed last night?
His cheeks burned with frustration. But what could he do?
Even if he complained and the culprits were punished, they'd
still wait for him outside. They'd hurt him. It had happened
before.

"*Amo te*, Daphne."

Ignore them, he thought.

"*Amo te*, Daphne."

Just stick to your work.

"*Amo te*—"

That was it. He could stand it no longer.

"Shut up!" he cried. "Shut up, you bastards!"

"Don't be like that, Daphne. Give us a kiss."

"Ah hem." Mr. Hamilton-Smythe looked up from his desk. "What seems to be the trouble, Daphne?"

"Nothing, sir."

"That was a very loud outburst."

"A paper cut, sir. My apologies."

"You're certain?"

Daphne pleaded with his eyes. Let it go. Drop it. You'll only make it worse.

"I'm positive, sir."

"All right. Class, please turn to page . . ."

Mr. Hamilton-Smythe led them through a piece of actual Latin prose. At first it was dull, then suddenly it was not. It seemed the author, a guy named Seneca, had been walking through the city one day when he spotted a bunch of prisoners being hauled to the Colosseum in a wagon. They were going to face the lions, and they knew it. One of the prisoners didn't like the idea. So he leaned over the side and put his head through the spokes of a wheel. The turning of the wheel snapped his neck.

Daphne wished he had the same courage.

When the period was over, Mr. Hamilton-Smythe asked Daphne to stay late. He stared at his books while his classmates walked out. He didn't need to see their faces to know they were silently warning him.

Mr. Hamilton-Smythe closed the door.

"Don't worry," he said kindly. "I know how it is. I won't ask you to say anything you don't want to."

"Thank you, sir."

"In fact, I'd like to give you an opportunity."

"Sir?"

"Sometimes, when it really seems as if the world is out to get you, the best way to help yourself is to help someone else."

"You're joking."

"Not at all." Mr. Hamilton-Smythe grinned. "The fact is, I'd like you to help *me*."

The Hamilton-Smythe apartment always made him feel itchy and lonesome—as if the elderly couple lived in a funeral home, or some haunted wax museum. The Victorian furniture was dark and heavy, with rotten coverings and tufts of horsehair sticking through the wounds. Thousands of books overflowed their shelves and lay in dusty, precarious mounds. Tables were adorned with cut-crystal figurines and tiny photographs in pewter frames. What made the experience so especially horrible was the odor of creams and medicines for all the strange ailments that old people acquired. The afterlife, Daphne was certain, stank of menthol.

"Here we are. I'm home, Elizabeth!"

Mr. H. offered him a chair across from Mrs. Hamilton-Smythe and went to the kitchen for a "nice refreshment." This turned out to be chocolate cake and lukewarm lemonade (as if somehow these foods were not repulsive together). Daphne tried not to stare at the vacant woman as he forced down the mouth-numbing combination. *She*, of course, did not mind staring at *him*. He wondered what Mr. H. would think if he just excused himself and left—just dropped out of Stoney Batter and became a hobo for the rest of his life. But he knew he'd never do it. Who did he think he was—MacInnes?

"Let me take your plate," the old man said politely.

Daphne was astonished to discover he'd swallowed every bite without gagging. Mr. H. returned with more lemonade. Ironically, the first glass had left Daphne so thirsty he had no choice but to drink this one as well. And then another. And still another. Until finally—

"I'm afraid that's the end of it," Mr. H. mourned. "Give me a few minutes, and I'll squeeze us another—"

"No!" Daphne cried. "I mean, water's fine."

"You're sure?"

"Positive."

"As you wish."

And then came the moment of truth.

"Elizabeth," the old man said, "I must run some errands. This young man has offered to read to you. Doesn't that sound nice?"

Mrs. Hamilton-Smythe blinked at the air.

"I knew you'd think so." The old man gave Daphne a lapful of cracked, moldy volumes. "I think you'll enjoy these," he said.

Daphne glanced at the titles hopefully. *Rasselas, Pierre, The Last of the Mohicans*. He was doomed.

"Have fun, you two!"

"Wait!" Daphne started to holler, but the door slammed shut, and that was that.

Imagine spending all eternity locked up with your grandmother's effigy. Daphne's heart beat so hard he had to loosen his collar and necktie.

"What shall we read first?" he said.

The zombie-woman stared at him.

"That Johnson fellow was a lot of laughs. Should we try him?"

Blink, blink. Stare, stare.

"You're not going to hurt me, are you?"

Nothing.

"Oh, God," he said. "Oh, God."

And then he was struck by a flash of genius. From the inner pocket of his school jacket he pulled the latest issue of *Dead Eye* magazine. The featured story was about the continuing escapades of "Capt. John Blaze, Explorer." He showed her the cover—and was shocked when her lips seemed to move. It wasn't much. Probably an idle breeze. But it might have been a smile.

"This is horrible stuff," he confessed. "My grandmother says it'll stunt my growth and turn me into a socialist."

Her lips moved again. This time there was no doubt.

"All right!" he said. "Captain John Blaze it is!"

The rest of the hour seemed to fly by as Capt. John Blaze explored the Peruvian jungles and battled the natives with his ringing machete. Almost before he knew it, Mr. H. was hanging his topcoat and cane on a rack by the door.

"How did it go?"

"Terrific!" Daphne said.

"Tell me, which book did you read?"

"Er—the one about the Indians."

Mr. H. smiled nostalgically.

"James Fenimore Cooper! Elizabeth and I used to read that to each other—back when we were courting."

Daphne tried to imagine the youthful couple—but could

not. Mr. H. had been old forever, it seemed. As for his wife: could she really have been a vital girl, a blushing bride, a doting spouse? To look at her now, it seemed impossible.

"I know," the old man said as if reading his thoughts. "That must seem like a very long time ago. Let me assure you it was. The world was different. Young people today have lost their sense of romance—of mystery and wonder. Everything has to be fast, or you want nothing to do with it. I'm sure you've spooned with quite a few young ladies, am I right?"

"Well . . ."

"Of course you have! Why, if I were your age . . . But never mind. I'm boring you to death. Here's a quarter. Take your chums down to the motion picture."

"Thank you, sir."

"I can't tell you how much I appreciate this, Daphne. Would you come back tomorrow?"

"Yes, sir. That would be very nice."

By now, the old man was practically in tears.

"Do you hear that, Elizabeth? You've made a new friend!"

10

Much have I travel'd in the realms of gold.

—JOHN KEATS

MacInnes spent the rest of the week attending classes, writing poems, and trying to ignore his conscience. He had a debt to settle, and it was bugging the hell out of him. (He might be a scoundrel, but at least he was an honorable one.)

Thus, Friday afternoon found him walking through the village, where he promptly got lost, and he was obliged to ask directions from the tobacconist. Puffing a five-cent cigar, he made his way into the industrial side of town: the stockyards, the tannery, the feed mill, the dump. He knew he was close when the streets turned to mud.

MacInnes had come to the icehouse. In the adjoining stable, the iceman was brushing his horse.

"That was some accident the other day," MacInnes commented.

"Lousy kids," the man growled. "Always in a hurry."

"Is the horse all right?"

"William Tell? He's fine. A little spooked is all."

MacInnes nodded stupidly. "Did you lose a lot of ice?"

"Twenty dollars' worth! That may not seem like a lot to you Academy boys, but to me it's a week's earnings."

Despite the iceman's opinion of "Academy boys," MacInnes had a pretty good idea what twenty dollars was worth. He took out his wallet and counted a wad of bills. When he was finished, all that remained was a single dollar and a tin of Ramses condoms.

"Here." He held out the money. "I hope this covers it."

The iceman frowned.

"The day I need a rich boy's charity is the day hell freezes over and puts Tom Gropek out of business."

"I'm not rich," MacInnes said quietly. "And it's not exactly charity. More like an apology."

Mr. Gropek held his gaze for a minute before taking the money and tucking it into a leather apron. Then he went back to brushing the horse. William Tell snorted and stamped a hoof.

"Easy, boy," the iceman said. And then, to MacInnes, "There's some carrots over there. William Tell might want a snack."

"Will he bite me?"

"Just keep your fingers out of his mouth."

MacInnes found the carrots and fed the horse.

"You covering for somebody, young man?"

"No, sir. I just like to play square."

Mr. Gropek nodded. "That took some guts, coming down here. Mind, I'm not saying that makes it okay to run folks off the road. Just that most kids would've pretended it was nothing."

"I tried that," MacInnes said. "It didn't take."

"You a scholarship boy?"

"Yes, sir."

"You need some part-time work, you come see me first. I don't pay much, but it's honest money."

"Yes, sir."

"Now hit the road before I change my mind and call the cops."

"Yes, sir."

"And don't be in such a damned hurry next time!"

The most direct route back to campus was by an unpaved road that cut through some cornfields before disappearing into the woods. MacInnes walked happily. Between puffs on his cigar, he whistled every song he knew—and quite a few that he didn't. As he drew closer to the school, he noticed a small red roadster parked inside the hollow of a curve. The lettering on the hood read BUGATTI. He knew next to nothing about automobiles, but what he did know suggested this was no ordinary car. Its owner must be either a tycoon or a thief.

He was about to walk on when he heard a girl sobbing.

"You're hurting me," she said. "Stop it."

"You don't really mean that," a deeper voice said.

"I do so mean it. Honestly, what's come over you?"

"Nothing's come over me. Weeks and weeks of nothing."

MacInnes placed his cigar on a tree branch and tiptoed into the woods. He quickly came to a clearing. The hairs on the back of his neck stood up when he recognized the ruined cottage where he'd met—or imagined—Miss Dubois. On the other side of the clearing, Trent Bloxom (who else?) had trapped a girl next to a tree. She was beautiful, MacInnes couldn't help noticing. She wore driving clothes, and though her hair was sensibly short, she hadn't spoiled it with the ridiculous water waves favored by most girls her age.

Bloxom held her by the wrists, crowding himself against the front of her pants.

"Please, Trent. We've been through all that."

"But I need you, Laura. You don't know what it does to me."

"I don't care what it does to you. Stop it."

MacInnes tramped across the clearing. "I'm pretty sure she means it, chum."

Bloxom turned his head. "MacInnes! Where did you come from?"

"I fell off an oyster boat."

"Eh? Never mind. This is none of your business."

"The young lady asked you to stop. I don't know all the local customs yet, but in my book that makes it my business."

"Then you've obviously misunderstood. Tell him, Laura."

"I . . ."

"Go on, Laura. Tell him it's a game we like to play."

MacInnes stepped closer. "Do you want me to leave you alone with him, miss?"

She shook her head. A tear glittered down her face.

"That's good enough for me, chum. Time to let her go."

"Of course."

MacInnes should have known it was too easy. Bloxom released his hold on Laura's wrists and backed away from the tree. The next thing MacInnes knew, he was sitting in the dirt and his jaw was numb.

Bloxom had actually punched him.

"You damned fool," MacInnes said.

"Are you all right?" Laura ran to his side. "I swear, Trent Bloxom, you must be the biggest ass alive."

She stooped to help MacInnes stand up, and accidentally tore a sleeve right off his blazer.

"Oh, my gosh! I'm terribly sorry."

"It's an old jacket," MacInnes said.

"Come on!" Bloxom hollered. He found a heavy stick and held it over his head. "Let's see what you're made of."

"I don't want to fight you," MacInnes said.

"What makes you think you have a choice?"

"You'll lose," MacInnes warned him.

"Like hell I will."

Bloxom stepped forward and brought down his weapon. MacInnes dodged it easily and threw a simple uppercut. The punch found Bloxom's nose, and the damned fool dropped like a stone.

"You don't spend your life in an orphanage without picking up a few things," MacInnes muttered.

"Son of a bitch!" Bloxom wailed. "You broke my nose! Get 'im, Laura. Kick 'im or something."

"Kick him yourself."

"Damn it, Laura!"

"Oh, grow up, Trent."

Bloxom's face looked like a dash of red paint. He put his arms out to steady himself and tried to stand up.

"I'll kill that son of a bitch!"

It was then that the voice interrupted them:

"I think that's enough violence, Mr. Bloxom."

"Dean Reverend," Bloxom whispered.

The old priest stood near the ruins. How long had he watched them?

"Sir," MacInnes said. "I think you should know—"

"Not now, MacInnes."

The Dean Reverend turned to Laura. "Young lady, I assume you attend the Hood School."

"Yes, sir."

"Then your presence here is a violation of your honor code. I suggest you leave immediately."

"Yes, sir."

"As for you boys—we'll discuss this after dinner."

Daphne sat in a large black willow overlooking the practice field. It was a lush, green tree with heavy branches perfect for sitting. He came here when he wanted to read in peace. The latest issue of *Terrible Tales* had arrived in the mail this morning, and just now he was reading a story about fish-eyed monsters who were scheming to take over the earth. But every now and then, when he felt he'd earned it, he glanced at the action below. Brian Alder, the Stoney Batter quarterback, was probably the most heroic-looking boy he'd ever seen. With his windswept hair and dashing jaw—who wouldn't want to look at him?

"Hello, up there!"

Daphne nearly dropped his magazine. No one knew he was here.

"Come on, Daphne. I saw you from the tower."

"Roger?"

"In the flesh. Aren't you going to invite me up?"

"Is anyone with you?"

"MacInnes is running an errand."

"What about anyone else?"

"You're the only other person I know."

"Oh. Yeah, come on up."

A minute later Roger was perched on a nearby branch.

"All right," he said. "Who are you hiding from?"

"What do you mean?"

"Oh, cut that out. You know what I mean."

Daphne wet his lips and decided he liked Roger's company. He didn't want him to go. And that meant telling him the truth.

"Everyone," he said. "I'm hiding from everyone."

"Is it really that bad?"

"You don't know the half of it. I spent all last year hiding in places like this. There's a bunch of guys in Marshall House who like to beat me up. Of course, the guys in Craxton House aren't much better."

"Is that why you skipped the Dean Reverend's Welcome?"

"Yeah. Pretty stupid, eh?"

Roger smiled and shook his head.

Daphne smiled back at him. "Am I really the only other person you know?"

"I keep to myself a lot."

"But you seem so—"

"—normal?"

"Yeah."

They sat quietly and watched the gridiron for a while. Brian Alder called a huddle. The players lined up, the ball was snapped, and Alder faded into the backfield. Just when he was about to be squashed by Edgar Sykes, he threw a forward pass. The ball sailed into the arms of Davey Byrd. Byrd dropped his shoulder and mowed down everyone who got between him and the goal.

Daphne sighed.

"I wish I played football," he said.

"Why's that?"

"So I could be part of something."

"But you're a part of something now," Roger said. "The most important part of all."

"Quit teasing me."

"I mean it."

"Well?"

"You're the part that studies the rest of the parts. The part that tries to make sense of it all. You're a philosopher."

"I am?"

"We all are. You, me, MacInnes."

"What if I want to be a different part?"

"Do you, though? Do you want to go through life worried about your socks and your hair, and whether you've been invited to all the right parties, and choosing your friends because they know all the right people? Is that what you want?"

"I thought I did. But the way you tell it—now I'm not sure."

Roger rubbed his chin. "I'll bet you know your way around," he said thoughtfully.

"If there's a place to hide, I know it."

"Maybe you can help me find some stuff."

"Like what?"

Roger searched his pocket and handed Daphne a list:

> 1 bicycle
> 1 large fan
> 1 sewing machine
> 50 bedsheets
> misc. pieces lumber

"I was right the first time. You really are crazy."

"Can you help me or not?"

"Well . . ." Daphne worked his jaw thoughtfully. "I might be able to put my hands on a bike no one's using . . ."

11

Near where the charter'd Thames does flow . . .
—WILLIAM BLAKE

After a meal of fatty ham and boiled potatoes, MacInnes walked to Roderick Hall. Its damp, gray stones gave the place all the appeal of a burial vault. Inside, it was no friendlier. Tall ceilings of dark, greasy wood seemed to swallow what feeble light was thrown by wrought-iron sconces. He found the Dean Reverend's outer office and waited in a stiff oak chair. The door to the inner office was open. In plain sight was Trent Bloxom, who looked so terrified that MacInnes couldn't help taking pity. The Dean Reverend himself remained hidden, sitting in ambush behind a monstrous desk. But there was no mistaking his gravelly voice:

"Well?" he said. "What do you have to say for yourself?"

"S-sir," Bloxom stammered. "Miss Waverly and I were having a private conversation—"

"Conversation! You threaten a young lady's virtue and call it a conversation?"

"Sir! With all due respect, I did no such thing."

"No?"

"I admit, it might have looked that way—from a distance. But I assure you, my intentions were innocent. If you don't believe me, ask Miss Waverly."

"As it happens," the Dean Reverend said, "I telephoned the Hood School during dinner. Miss Waverly has verified your story."

"Then—"

"She's lying, of course. Apparently, she feels some sort of obligation to you. No matter. The events speak for themselves. I know what I saw, and I know what I heard."

In the silence that followed, a skeletal hand reached across the desk and pointed to a display of photographs on the wall: grim young chaps in school-striped ties. To MacInnes, they looked like the portraits of criminals he'd seen in the post office.

"Discipline and sacrifice," the Dean Reverend said. "That's what it comes down to. Working hard and playing by the rules. Any idea who these boys are?"

"Er—Stoney Batter graduates?"

"Not just graduates! The cream of the crop! The boys on this wall attended the most prestigious colleges in the country. Yale. Harvard. Princeton. That fellow with the big ears went on to be a state senator."

The Dean Reverend paused for dramatic effect.

"Any idea what it takes to be so successful?"

"Discipline and sacrifice?"

"Exactly! Sloth, drunkenness, lust, vengeance: these are the forces that tempt us to the brink of the vortex. Take one step too many, and not even the hand of God will bear you up. Most of these boys left Stoney Batter with unblemished records. A few may have strayed once or twice—but rest assured they soon realized their peril and never strayed again. And now the choice is yours. Do you follow their example and take the path that leads to greatness? Or do you take the path that leads into the vortex of evil?"

"Please, sir." Bloxom's whole body shook. "I *am* sorry."

"Sorrow is easy. It's your salvation I'm worried about."

"Sir?"

"Are you willing to make a sacrifice?"

At first, Bloxom looked bewildered. Then the light dawned. A bronze rail was bolted to the wall. He went to it and unbuttoned his trousers. He hitched up his blazer, gripped the rail, and thrust out his bare buttocks. The Dean Reverend came into view. In his fist was a wooden paddle that had been varnished to a gloss with the sweat of countless boys.

MacInnes bit his lip. He was no friend of Bloxom's, that was sure. But no one deserved *this*.

"Our Father," the Dean Reverend said, and Bloxom joined him for the rest, "Who art in Heaven . . ."

MacInnes winced with every whack of the paddle.

". . . forever and ever. Amen."

When he looked up, the Dean Reverend had vanished again, and Bloxom was buttoning his trousers.

"How do you feel?"

"Sir?"

"Do you feel cleansed? Has the evil fled your soul?"

"Yes, sir."

"I wish I could be as certain."

"But, sir—what else can I *do*?"

"Why, Good Works, of course. You'd like that, wouldn't

you? A chance to do something constructive for the old school?"

Bloxom nodded. His face was wet with tears. A ribbon of fresh blood ran from his swollen nose.

"That's the spirit! The only problem is, school hasn't been in session long enough for anything to need fixing. Tell you what. Let's wait a few weeks and see what turns up, eh?"

"Yes, sir."

"And, Bloxom? Stay away from Miss Waverly for a while."

"But—!"

"You may escort her to the Fall Cotillion if you wish—assuming she'll have you."

"Yes, sir."

Bloxom limped into the outer office. His eyes met MacInnes's for a long, frantic moment. Then he started out.

"Wait," MacInnes said.

"Get lost, you faggot."

MacInnes held out a handkerchief. Bloxom snatched it away.

"Thanks," he said gruffly.

MacInnes crept into the inner office. The Dean Reverend was at his desk, making notes in a ledger. MacInnes took in his surroundings: the photos of graduates, a rack of clerical vestments, the Book of Common Prayer lying open on a table. The wall behind the desk was dominated by a massive crucifix. A figure of the Savior was nailed to the planks in garish detail. A bit High Church for a boys' school, wasn't it? Who *was* this Dean Reverend anyway?

Finally, the codger looked up.

"Thank you for coming, MacInnes. After our dialogue in class, I envisioned a meeting like this. I did not imagine it would occur so soon."

"No, sir."

"What were you doing on that road anyway?"

"Just taking a walk, sir. Finding my way around."

"Lucky thing. I shudder to think what might have happened if you hadn't intervened on the young lady's behalf."

"Then you know—"

"Everything, MacInnes. You protected that girl, and then you protected yourself. Is that the way you remember it?"

"Yes, sir."

"And you weren't deliberately looking for trouble? You had no foreknowledge of Mr. Bloxom's intent?"

MacInnes settled for a half-truth.

"No, sir."

"Well, as I said, it was a lucky thing. And a very honorable response on your part. You're to be congratulated."

"Thank you, sir."

"On the other hand," the Dean Reverend said, "Stoney Batter does not tolerate fighting under any circumstances."

"Not even in self-defense?"

"Order must be maintained."

MacInnes thought about launching a fierce rebuttal, but he'd witnessed the Dean Reverend's insane brand of logic, and he knew it would get him nowhere.

"Would you like to beat me, sir?"

"I don't think so. Consider yourself on probation. It's my experience that boys who know how to fight often create situations in which they need to. Enough said?"

"Yes, sir."

"Very well, then. Good night, MacInnes."

"Good night, sir."

What kind of school was this anyway? He almost wished he *had* been expelled.

He wandered through the twilight and hoped no one would see him. Some chaps on the other side of the quad were goofing around with a football—laughing, making jokes. Suddenly, the ball flew in his direction. He snatched it from the air and threw it back in a single fluid motion. He knew without looking that the ball would go exactly where he aimed it. He'd played a little football at the orphanage, but the daily scrimmages had kept him from his writing, so he'd given the game up entirely. He hadn't missed it, either.

"Holy cow!" said one of the chaps.

"Say, fella!" called the other. "That's some throw you have. Ever think of going out for the team?"

"No."

"You sure? Coach Curran would blah blah blah . . ."

MacInnes ignored them and kept walking. He was halfway to Craxton House, and ready for a smoke, when he heard the growl of a motor. He turned, and a familiar red roadster stopped beside him, kicking up tufts of lawn.

"You're a hard man to find," the driver said as she raised her goggles. "I've left tire tracks all over campus."

His heart skipped a beat. "What are you doing here?" he said. "Don't you have a curfew or something?"

"I have enough time," she said. "Anyway, this is important."

"Oh?"

"I suppose I should introduce myself. I'm Laura Waverly."

"Yes, I know. I'm Michael MacInnes."

"I'm here because I never properly thanked you."

"That's really not necessary, Miss Waverly."

"I think it is. And call me Laura."

She smiled. Her teeth were very white, and with curls of hair peeking out from her cap, she looked even prettier than before. Not being held captive probably added to the effect.

"Look," he said. "It's none of my business—"

"You want to know why I go around with Trent?"

"Something like that."

"Would it surprise you if I said I don't know?"

"Stop doing it, then."

"It's not that simple. Trent has his good side. And he's an old friend of the family."

"Are you in love with him?"

She laughed. "You really get to the point, don't you?"

"Etiquette confuses me. I'd rather just talk to people."

"A refreshing philosophy."

"So, are you? In love with Bloxom, I mean."

"No."

"But you lied to protect him."

"You know about that?"

"The Dean Reverend is very efficient."

"Ah. Well, the truth is, I didn't really lie. You see, I've known Trent most of my life. And what he did to me—that is, what he was threatening to do—it's not like him. He was overwhelmed by the moment, that's all. So when I spoke to your Dean Reverend, I told him about the real Trent—the way he normally is. That's not lying, is it?"

MacInnes could have said a few things about the "real Trent," but he was already half in love with the girl, and if she was ever going to love him in return, he didn't want it to be because he'd tattled on a rival.

"I suppose not" was his only comment.

"Anyway," she said. "I have something for you."

She handed him a large, gift-wrapped package.

"What's this?" he asked.

"A reward."

He unwrapped it. Inside was a new school blazer. Even in the twilight he knew the fabric and workmanship were three times the quality of the one she'd accidentally torn.

"It's beautiful," he said.

"Try it on."

He did. It was a perfect fit.

"Uh-oh," she said. "You have a loose thread. Let me see."

He bent forward, and she kissed him. Loose thread indeed!

"I have to go," she said, and the Bugatti rumbled to life.

"May I see you again?" he hollered over the noise.

"Look for me at the Fall Cotillion!" She put her goggles back on and sped wildly into the night.

He watched in dumb amazement.

It was only later, as he was getting ready for bed, that he wondered if Miss Dubois's prophecy was coming true after all.

12

After short silence then,
And summons read, the great consult began.
—JOHN MILTON

A month passed. The days grew cool, the leaves began to turn. The campus was a frenzy of color: gentian, gold, vermilion, dung. It was a good season for writing, and MacInnes submitted poem after poem to the *Review*. Naturally, each was rejected out of hand. Bloxom's comments were succinct. *Vulgar. Blasphemous. Written by an idiot. No respect for tradition.* MacInnes's only gratification came during Mr. Moffett's class, where he was able to observe the metamorphosis of Bloxom's nose. It too changed colors on a daily basis, and when it was healed, it was decidedly mashed and crooked.

Roger, meanwhile, had developed a habit of visiting God Knew Where and stealing armloads of junk, which he stashed in sinister piles around the tower. He claimed it was "scientific apparatus," but MacInnes knew better.

"Enough is enough," he said one Saturday afternoon. "What're you planning to do with all this junk?"

"What junk?"

"Don't 'what junk?' me, old chum. This place is starting to look like a flea market."

"Just you wait," Roger said. "One of my inventions will save your life one day, and then you won't be so smug."

"How're you going to save my life with a broken bicycle?"

"It's not broken. It's dismantled."

"Does it work?"

"Not at the moment—"

"Then it's broken."

"Aargh! Has anyone ever mentioned how frustrating you are?"

"All the time, chum. All the time."

At long last, Capt. John Blaze hacked his way out of the jungle. He bade farewell to his Peruvian mistress and drifted out to sea for yet another adventure.

Daphne closed his magazine and wondered what he would read to Mrs. Hamilton-Smythe while they waited for the next installment.

"My God!" The door slammed behind him. "What have you done?"

Daphne panicked. Mr. H. strode into the sitting room without bothering to hang up his coat. This was going to get ugly.

"Please, sir," Daphne begged. "I know you wanted me to read all that Fenimore Cooper stuff, but I just couldn't—"

"My dear boy, *forget* the Cooper! Elizabeth is smiling!"

It was true. Every time he'd come by to read, her smile

had grown just a little bit more. Daphne had begun to take it for granted.

"Doesn't she smile when you read to her, sir?"

"To the best of my knowledge, she hasn't smiled at anything in the last three years."

"I didn't realize."

"Well, of course you didn't! Nobody did! Dr. Cornwell swore she was gone—but she's only been biding her time!"

Mr. H. knelt before his wife. "Elizabeth, do you like this young man?"

Her nod was nearly imperceptible. But it was there.

"Do you like this wild stuff he's been reading you?"

Another small nod.

"Daphne—that book of yours—would you lend it to me?"

"Heck, I'll give it to you. It's just a stupid magazine."

"Stupid? It's a work of genius. And you, my boy, are one of God's angels. Now, please—leave me alone with her."

Daphne went upstairs and found that his roommate, Charlie Schlage, was sponsoring an illicit game of skittles. The whirl of the top, the clatter of pins. Charlie and his chums leered over the skittle board, swigging Entwistle's liquor and crunching onion sandwiches till the tears ran down their cheeks.

Every morsel of happiness that Daphne had felt disappeared.

"All rightie, fellows," Charlie said. "Place yer bets."

Cigarette halves and sticks of gum were dropped inside a hat.

"Now, stand back, gentlemen. I'm about to set a record!"

Charlie placed the top on the board and yanked the string.

The top spun off, gracefully winding from one chamber to the next, knocking over pin after pin. The drunken boys looked on. When the top finally came to a rest, not a single pin remained standing.

"Cripes!" a boy exclaimed.

"Didja see how hard he pulled the string?"

"Naw, the trick's in how he winds it."

"You dopes," Daphne blurted. "It's all random chance."

Charlie threw a book at him. "Get lost, you dumbbell."

"You can't make me," Daphne protested. "It's my room too."

"So, what're you going to do about it? Mr. Hamilton-Belch isn't here to protect you."

"I—"

"Yeah?"

Daphne left. He went down to the lav, found an empty stall, and tried to vanquish his despair in the only way he knew how. At first he tried thinking of Clara Bow, the movie star. Then he got confused, and his fantasy took on the features of Roger Legrande. He'd known this would happen. His obsession with pulp magazines had finally led him astray. The worst of his grandmother's fears had come true. He was a pervert! A fiend! He was out of control! His forearm flew as if it had a mind of its own!

"Good heavens, Edgar. Look at what the world is coming to."

"It's a dirty disgrace. Someone should do something."

"My sentiments exactly. But who?"

"I believe it is the proctor's responsibility."

"Ah! So it is—"

Daphne was scrambling to cover himself—to hide the evidence of his sin—but it was far too late for that. Entwistle and Sykes had seen everything. The fat proctor held the door that Daphne had somehow forgotten to latch. His stupid friend was simply gloating.

For once, the future was clear. Daphne was going to die. His death would be sensational. Stoney Batter boys for generations to come would pass the tale on. His name would be legend. But he was still going to die.

Sykes hauled him from the toilet with his knickers still bunched around his ankles.

"Let me go, you bastard!"

Entwistle regarded him grimly. "The house charges you, Daphne, with unlawful masturbation and homosexual tendencies. How do you plead?"

"I'm not saying anything!"

"The house finds you guilty. Edgar"—smiling—"bring him."

Upstairs in the tower, MacInnes was glancing at the first issue of *The Stoney Batter Review*. The essays were trivial, the stories were plagiarized, and the poems were cluttered with thees and thous and red, red roses. Bloxom's own contribution was entitled "Ode to a Football Hero." The first few lines were enough to turn MacInnes's stomach:

The boy stood on the muddy field.
The orb was in his hand.
And when he ducked his head and charged
A thrill rushed through the fans.

Codswallop, he thought. Undiluted codswallop!

"Do you know what this is?" he said to Roger.

"Codswallop?"

"Offal."

"Excrement?"

"Smirch."

He tossed the magazine into the coal stove and set it ablaze. While he was there, he risked a peek at Roger's work. As far as he could tell, his roommate had connected a bicycle chain to an old fan mechanism. Pedaling the bicycle would cause the fan blades to spin. But why?

He never got the chance to ask. A cheer broke out downstairs.

"What's all that?" MacInnes said.

"One of Entwistle's parties, I suppose."

"Well, it's damned annoying. What if I were writing my speech for the Quintilian Oratory?"

"Are you?"

"Of course not."

Another cheer wafted up from below.

"You're right," Roger said. "It's annoying."

"So what are we waiting for?"

A crowd had gathered at the end of the hall. Half the residents of the house were there. What they were gawking at, MacInnes couldn't guess. They were waiting for something. Whenever it happened, they cheered.

"I don't like it," MacInnes said.

"Me neither."

"Can you see Daphne anywhere?"

"Oh, Christ. You don't think—"

"Daphne!" MacInnes called.

The crowd looked angrily at the interruption.

"Ah!" Entwistle exclaimed. "The new boys have arrived."

"What have you done with him?" Roger said.

Entwistle waved his hand imperiously, and the crowd stepped aside. At the center of the makeshift arena, Daphne was tied to a wooden chair. His shirt was torn, his knickers were down, and his spectacles were nowhere in sight. He was sobbing.

"Behold the price of disobedience," Entwistle said.

Sykes pinched Daphne's nostrils. Daphne squirmed drunkenly, fighting for air. When his mouth finally opened, Sykes filled it with Entwistle's moonshine and clamped it shut until the smaller boy swallowed. Only then did he let Daphne breathe.

The crowd cheered.

MacInnes felt sick. He started toward Entwistle, ready to kill him, but someone locked his arms in a wrestling hold. He looked around, and Roger was caught too. They were helpless.

"You coward," he said. "Why're you doing this?"

"Onanism," Entwistle explained, "is a sin against God."

"Damned right," someone agreed.

"Should've just dropped him out the window."

"Lousy faggot." This from Charlie Schlage.

"Onanism?" MacInnes couldn't believe it. "You're kidding me, right?"

"Justice has been served," Entwistle said. "It's tradition."

"It's medieval."

"It's a Stoney Batter custom. Your little chum knew the risk when he unfastened his belt. He made his own choice. And now he's paid the price."

"He's right," Daphne sputtered. "I knew it was wrong."

"My God." MacInnes was awestruck. "You've got him trained!"

"Hardly," Entwistle said. "If that were true, he would never have been playing with himself."

"So what's the crime in playing with yourself?" Roger said.

The mob stared at him as if he were crazy.

"What's the crime—!"

"He must be another one!"

"Didn't you know? He and MacInnes are homosexuals too!"

"Who can tell what goes on in that tower of theirs?"

MacInnes strained against the arms that held him.

"Everyone masturbates!" he shouted. "It's only natural. I dare any one of you to look me in the eye and say you never did it. Come on! I dare you!"

One by one, the boys looked at their feet. Even Entwistle could only gnaw at the inner flesh of his cheek, and for a moment it seemed MacInnes might triumph. But then—

"So what?" said Charlie Schlage. "So what if we've all done it? That doesn't make it right. It's still antisocial."

"Gentlemen," Entwistle said, regaining confidence. "The show is over. Let us retire to our rooms."

After some grumbling, the mob dispersed.

"I did warn you," Entwistle said. And then he was gone too.

Roger and MacInnes knelt over Daphne. A shiner had blossomed under his left eye, and his lower lip was bleeding. MacInnes licked his shirtsleeve and wiped Daphne's face.

"My specs!" Daphne was bawling. "What'll I do?"

"I'll find them," Roger said.

"Wait!" Daphne cried. "Don't leave me!"

"It's okay. I'll be right back."

MacInnes walked Daphne to the lav and applied the universal treatment: he helped him throw up.

Then they went up to the tower. He lent Daphne some clothes and let him rest on his bunk. Feeling out of his depth, he put his hand on Daphne's forehead. The kid was ice-cold. Now what?

Roger came in with Daphne's spectacles and shrugged. He took them to his workbench and fired up a soldering torch.

"Oh, God," Daphne moaned. "I feel awful."

"Have you ever been drunk before?" MacInnes said.

"Is that what I am? How long does it last?"

"A few hours. Maybe all night."

"Why are you helping me? I'm disgusting. Don't you hate me?"

"Of course not."

"But there's something wrong with me. The other fellows—"

"The other fellows are full of shit. Everyone masturbates."

Daphne's lip trembled. "Even you?"

"Sometimes."

"What about Roger?"

"Afraid so," Roger admitted.

"Think of it as practice," MacInnes said. "One day you'll be with a girl, and . . ."

Daphne closed his eyes.

"That is"—MacInnes flushed—"assuming you like girls."

"I don't know what I like."

Silence filled the tower. Roger ended it by giving Daphne his spectacles. Miraculously, the lenses had survived. The earpieces had not, though, and Roger had soldered clumsy pieces of wire in their place. Daphne didn't seem to mind. He put on the spectacles and heaved a sigh of relief.

"How do I look?"

"Like spaghetti and meatballs."

"What's wrong with the lenses?"

Roger and MacInnes looked at each other.

"What do you mean?" Roger said.

"Everything's all fuzzy."

"You're drunk," MacInnes reminded him.

"Wait," Roger said. "Is it like a snowstorm?"

"Kinda. Like it's blowing all around me."

"How's your gut feel?"

"It hurts. Pretty bad."

Roger looked worried. He pulled MacInnes aside.

"What is it, chum?"

"I might be wrong, but I think it's wood-alcohol poisoning."

"Damned Entwistle," MacInnes said. "Should we take Daphne to the infirmary? I couldn't stand it if he went blind or something."

"There *is* a treatment," Roger said. "But I don't think Dr. Cornwell will give it to him."

"What is it?"

"Believe it or not, more alcohol. The good stuff, I mean. Do you have any?"

"Some brandy, sure. But how can more liquor be good for him?"

"Wood alcohol is methanol. Amateur distillers don't know how to keep it out. A little won't hurt, but too much can dilate the veins in your eyes till they burst. A little more, and your liver gives out."

"Coffin varnish . . ."

"Yeah. The good news is that ethanol—real liquor—replaces methanol in the bloodstream. Just boils it off. In fact, it's the only way I know to get rid of it."

"So if we pump him full of brandy—"

"—we'll be pumping the bad stuff out."

"He's not going to like it," MacInnes said.

"He doesn't have much choice."

"You tell him. He's taken a liking to you."

"Er—yeah."

Roger explained the situation, and Daphne started sobbing all over again.

"Just let me die," he begged.

They took turns watching him throughout the night. He flailed and tossed, and twice he woke up screaming. But in the morning, he was alive. His stomach had stopped hurting, and his vision was back to normal.

To celebrate, they all went down to Sunday breakfast—though Daphne chose not to eat.

"Entwistle's a goddamned menace," MacInnes said as he

chomped a piece of fatty ham. "How long before he kills someone?"

"What do you want to do?" Roger said.

"Put him out of business, what else?"

"Well, sure. Why didn't I think of that?"

"What's the problem, chum?"

"To put him out of business, we'll have to smash his supply."

"Yeah?"

"Do *you* know where he keeps it?"

"I assumed it was in his room."

Roger shook his head. "Tell him, Daphne."

"Entwistle's terrified Mr. Hamilton-Smythe might find it," Daphne explained. "So he keeps it hidden somewhere else."

"I don't suppose you know where?"

"You kidding?" Daphne said. "No one knows."

13

*I care not for these Ladies,
That must be wooed and prayed.*

—THOMAS CAMPION

Twice each year, in the fall and spring, Stoney Batter hosted a Grand Cotillion for the young ladies who attended the Hood School. No expense was spared, no exertion was too great. The dining hall was transformed into a glittering ballroom. Chefs were hired to roast enormous birds and steamship rounds of beef. Punches flowed from gorgeous fountains. A forty-piece orchestra played numbers by Strauss and Tchaikovsky. Debutantes were literally swept off their feet by young men in tuxedos. Jazz was forbidden, of course, as were Charlestons, shimmies, and fox-trots—but this did nothing to squash the delirium. Girls! Just think of it! They were going to meet girls! And if a fellow happened to meet just the right sort of girl, with the right sort of attitude—anything might happen!

"Count me out," Roger said.

"Me too," Daphne echoed.

"Oh, come on, chums," MacInnes said. "How bad can it be?"

"You'll find out," Roger said. "I've been to things like this before. Rich girls aren't happy just dancing with you, see. They want to interrogate you. Who's your family? Who are your friends? Where do you spend the summer?"

"He's right," Daphne said. "I went last year. It was awful."

MacInnes shrugged. "I'll take my chances."

Roger studied him. "Looking like that?"

"Like what?"

"Your hair's a disaster, for one thing. When's the last time you had it cut?"

"Well—"

"At least comb some brilliantine through it."

"Like one of those slicker boys? Never!"

"Where's your tuxedo, then?"

"What's wrong with the clothes I'm wearing?"

"You can't go to a cotillion in your school clothes!"

"We orphans don't keep extensive wardrobes."

"Oh."

"Besides which, this is the jacket Miss Waverly gave me."

"Oh, I get it." Roger smiled. "It's all about *her*."

"What you mean," Daphne said, "is it's all about sex."

"More than that!" MacInnes cried. "Sex is just a beginning: a way of opening windows and breaking down walls. Unscrew the locks from their doors! Unscrew the doors from their jambs! Something's out there, chums—it's waiting for me—I can feel it—the sublime sense of something more deeply interfused . . ."

MacInnes held Daphne by the shoulders. "Concentrate!" he ordered. "What do you feel?"

Daphne shut his eyes obediently and squeezed his face in deep thought. His entire body shuddered, and for a moment he looked as if he was about to have an inspiration. He sneezed instead.

"Anyway," MacInnes said. "She promised me a dance."

"How're you going to get around Bloxom?" Roger said.

"I shall leave it in the hands of fate."

When MacInnes had gone, Roger turned to Daphne and said, "Are you ready?"

"If being terrified means I'm ready—yes."

"You followed Sykes to the gymnasium, right?"

"Yeah. He's lifting weights. Just like always."

"Did he see you?"

"You kidding? He'd've killed me."

Roger looked at his watch. "It's almost time."

He crept to the foot of the tower stairs and cracked the hall door. At precisely seven-thirty, Howard Entwistle locked his room and walked down to the lav. He wore a bathrobe the size of a tent. A few minutes later, the shower started running.

"Why doesn't he shower with the rest of us?" Roger asked.

"He says he's too dignified."

"Too embarrassed is more like it."

"Not too embarrassed to go around torturing people."

Roger nodded. "You know your part?"

"Watch out for Sykes. If he comes, I scream the code word."

"Which is—?"

"Chop suey."

Roger sneaked into the lav. The shower was blasting away, and the air was thick with steam. He could barely see the cubbies, but it turned out not to matter. Entwistle's robe wasn't in one. He scanned them again, in case he'd missed it, before realizing his mistake. If Entwistle really was embarrassed, he wouldn't put his robe in a cubby. He'd wear it as long as he could.

Certain he was about to be caught, Roger moved closer to the shower. The robe was draped over a chair. He ran his fingers through the enormous garment until he found a pocket that bulged. This was it. He removed Entwistle's key ring as gently as he could. Still, a couple of keys jingled together.

"Who's there?" Entwistle called.

Roger backed up. He gripped the keys so hard the little teeth cut his skin.

"Is that you, Edgar?"

He had to say something before Entwistle got suspicious. He covered his mouth with his hand.

"It's Charlie," he mumbled.

"Schlage? What's the matter with your voice?"

"I'm brushing my teeth. You know, for the dance."

"Well, finish up. You know I bathe privately."

"Sorry, Howard."

He made a gargling sound and ran some water in the sink. Then he left.

Daphne was pacing the hall. "You took forever!" he complained.

"Tell me something I don't know. Any sign of Sykes?"

"None."

"It's on to step two, then."

Roger used the keys to unlock Entwistle's door. The room, he discovered, was furnished like a men's club, with leather chairs, inlaid tables, and prints of English castles. It was ridiculous. Who did Entwistle think he was—a railroad baron?

He found what he was looking for in the closet: two cases of Canadian whiskey. It seemed like a lot, but he knew there must be more. He carried them up to the tower.

"I'm going to be sick," Daphne said.

"Not yet," Roger warned him.

He locked Entwistle's room and returned the keys to the robe without incident.

"Oh, my gosh," Daphne said. "That was great. You were brilliant. It was like something out of *Detective Story Magazine*."

"You were pretty brilliant yourself."

"Naw, you did all the tricky stuff."

"You wouldn't think that if Sykes had come along."

"That's true." Daphne grinned. "I took a risk, didn't I?"

"Yup."

"So now what?"

"First we empty these bottles."

"And then—?"

"We wait."

Howard Entwistle was ecstatic. He loved cotillions. Not because he liked dancing—he wouldn't even attend—but because the company of young ladies inspired young men to get drunk. If things went well, he'd make a fortune tonight.

And the truly wonderful thing was that no one suspected.

Not the Dean Reverend, not even Mr. Hamilton-Smythe. The fat, pimpled proctor was above reproach!

Someone knocked on the door. Edgar showed a tuxedoed boy into the room.

"How may I help you?"

"I hear you sell things."

"That depends. What are you after?"

"Tarantula juice?"

Entwistle frowned. "Edgar, show this gentleman out."

"Huh?" The boy looked puzzled.

"I do not traffic in 'tarantula juice,'" Entwistle explained. "I sell nothing but imported goods. My stuff is the real McCoy."

"All right. How much?"

"Twenty dollars a quart."

"That's highway robbery! Not even Throckmorton—"

"Take it or leave it."

"All right, all right," handing over a bill.

"Edgar—?"

Sykes went to the closet. When he returned, he was scratching his head.

"I'll, uh, have to get it from the stash."

Entwistle's chest began to pound. Things were *not* going well.

"I thought you stocked the closet this morning."

"I thought I did too."

The boy in the tuxedo blinked his eyes nervously. "This is a joke, right?"

"Silence!" Entwistle cried. His ears were rushing. He needed some medicine. But later, later. "You'll get your liquor," he told the boy. "It will simply take a few minutes. Edgar?"

"I'm on my way, Howard."

"While we're waiting," Entwistle said, sliding open a drawer, "can I interest you in some photographs? French postcards, perhaps? We carry an extensive array of poses . . ."

Roger and Daphne watched Sykes leave the room.

"Here we go again," Roger whispered.

"What if he sees us?"

"We live here, remember? Anyway, they're the ones breaking the law, not us."

"I suppose."

They followed Sykes down the stairwell. Roger was sure he'd go out by the main door and they'd have to follow him over hill and dale, but Sykes never even glanced that way. He kept climbing down—to the cellar? Of course! Keep the liquor hidden, but keep it nearby.

With Daphne looking over his shoulder, Roger peeked around the corner. Sykes was halfway down the cellar hall. He opened a door and slipped inside.

"What's that place?" Roger said.

"The boiler room."

"Is there any way out?"

"I don't think so."

"That's it, then. That's where they're stashing the hooch."

They ducked into the laundry room and waited for Sykes to come back. They waited a long time.

"What's he doing?" Daphne said.

"He's just being careful. Doesn't want to get caught."

At last the door opened. Sykes emerged with a case of whiskey and lumbered back to the stairwell. Roger and Daphne waited a few minutes, just to be sure, and then retraced his steps.

The boiler room was dark. The ceiling was a confusion of pipes and valves, and the boilers cast eerie shadows. Roger tried a light switch, but the lamp was broken. Sykes had probably broken it himself.

"I'm getting the heebie-jeebies," Daphne said.

"You've been reading too many stories."

"Yeah. This is the part where the mutant crab slides out of its burrow and stings us with his tentacles—"

"—and then puts us on a spaceship for Mars?"

"You read that one too?"

"I've looked at a few. But that doesn't mean I believe them."

Once their eyes had grown accustomed to the darkness, they searched every crevice where a stash of bottles might fit. Daphne singed his eyebrows looking under the boilers, and Roger bumped his head looking between the pipes and the ceiling. Choking on a mouthful of dust, he got an idea.

"Dust!" he said. "We should follow Sykes's footprints."

"I could've told you that," Daphne said.

"So why didn't you?"

"Because it's bloody dark in here."

"It's not that dark."

But a glance at the floor proved that if Sykes had left any footprints, Roger and Daphne had erased them by now.

"There's nothing here," Roger said eventually.

"We saw Sykes carry out a box."

"What have we missed, then?"

"A secret passage? A hidden door? Another room?"

Roger laughed. "There you go with your stories again."

"So we're just giving up? After everything we went through?"

"You win some, you lose some."

"All I ever do is lose," Daphne said. "I really wanted to win this time."

"Cheer up. We came close. Maybe MacInnes can figure it out."

"I wish he was here now."

"Well, that's MacInnes for you. He's got his own priorities."

14

She walks in beauty, like the night
Of cloudless climes and starry skies . . .
—GEORGE GORDON, LORD BYRON

Nothing in the orphanage had prepared MacInnes for the opulence of the Grand Cotillion. The music, the lights, the potted ferns, the embroidered napkins—how had he ended up *here*? Boys he'd seen in the classroom looked like absolute strangers in their bow ties and starched white shirts. A bronze cupid sprayed a froth of lemonade six feet into the air. What amazed him the most was a pair of ice sculptures: scale miniatures of the Hood School and Stoney Batter campuses, meticulously carved to the finest detail, right down to the bricks and molding. He thought of all the labor some poor bastard had put into them, chipping away with picks and magnifying lenses—and here they were melting away from the heat of perspiring dancers. A card in front of the display read: GROPEK & SONS, ICE AND COLD STORAGE.

"Excuse me?"

MacInnes whirled around. Practically touching him was a very attractive girl with yellow hair bobbed so close to her scalp that a phrenologist could have read her bumps.

"Yes?"

"Do you want to dance?"

MacInnes smiled. "No, thank you."

The girl pouted and walked off. Clearly, she was not used to rejection.

MacInnes patrolled the ballroom, waiting for Miss Waverly to show up. She *had* promised him a dance, hadn't she? Or had she only said that she'd see him? He couldn't remember.

"They're striking up a waltz," another girl said behind him.

He turned. "Oh?"

"The orchestra's hittin' on all six, don'tcha think?"

He nodded in silence. Eventually she took the hint and looked for another partner.

As the minutes turned into an hour, MacInnes began to notice an interesting phenomenon. A mean-looking woman in a high-collared gown was occasionally stopping girls on the dance floor. She held a ruler, and at first MacInnes thought she was going to beat them. In fact, she was measuring the amount of leg exposed between each girl's hemline and the floor. He wondered why she hadn't done this at the Hood School gate, before they'd even left for Stoney Batter. Then he saw why. A number of girls had stitched false bottoms to their dresses—one yank of thread, and four more inches of stockinged calf were exposed to the world.

MacInnes admired their ingenuity. Hood School girls were no dopes.

Suddenly the impossible happened. Beyond the pale of decency, the orchestra tooted the first notes of a Charleston!

The applause was deafening. Dozens of couples leapt to the stage. Hips began to jiggle, elbows to flex, heels to stomp, and bodies to quiver like gelatin. One plucky fellow did flips through the air. Another gave lessons in the knock-kneed crossover step. A girl climbed a table and shrieked at the top of her lungs:

"Dance! Dance! Everyone dance the Charleston!"

At most, the orgy lasted a minute. That was how long it took the Dean Reverend and Mrs. Vanderlip (she of the ruler) to silence the orchestra and begin hollering through cardboard megaphones:

"Stop this animal behavior at once!"

"Think of your parents!"

"Think of the tragedy in Boston!"

"One more outburst like that, and the cotillion is over!"

"The next boy who tips the orchestra will be expelled!"

A collective sigh resounded through the ballroom.

"Shucks."

"Gee whiz."

"Aw, hooey."

MacInnes grew excited. They were going to start a revolution. They were going to fight for their liberties. They were going to behead the portly queen and her prudish prime minister. They were going to . . . mince quietly away and sip punch? The interruption was already forgotten. The orchestra played a proper one-step, and the dancers resumed their frigid embraces. MacInnes was outraged. Not for himself—but for the principle of the thing. Sheep, he thought. Following their authorities into the slaughterhouse, and never once questioning their mythology.

"Good evening, MacInnes," a familiar voice said.

"How are you, Mr. Hamilton-Smythe?"

"Disappointed."

"You too, eh?"

"They used to serve a wonderful cheesecake at these shindigs, but I can't seem to find any."

"Let's look together."

He took the old gentleman's elbow and steered him toward the dessert table.

"By the way, MacInnes. Have you started writing your speech for Craxton-Marshall Weekend?"

"I certainly have," MacInnes lied.

"Excellent! When will you have something to show me?"

"Well, I don't want to rush things, you know."

"Of course you don't. Take your time, get it right."

"Will next week—?"

"Ah!"

"You feeling okay, sir?"

"The cheesecake! And only one piece left! Out of my way—!"

Mr. Hamilton-Smythe started hobbling around the table, using his cane to jab the toes of anyone foolish enough to be in his path. MacInnes couldn't help laughing. How marvelous, he thought, that men like Mr. Hamilton-Smythe should even exist.

"Hi there!"

Standing beside him was a lovely girl who looked every inch the southern belle that her accent proclaimed her to be.

"Hi there, yourself," he responded.

"I'm Marjorie Culpepper. Wanna dance?"

"Um, well, you see, Miss Culpepper—"

"Call me Marjorie!" What she really said was "Maah-jrih."

"Marjorie. The thing is—"

"Forget the dance, handsome. Wanna go somewhere and pet?"

"I beg your pardon?"

"You heard me all right."

MacInnes looked at the short brown hair and lips so full he could kiss them right now. She was no Laura Waverly— but for all he knew, Laura hadn't even come tonight. And he'd already turned down so many others—who could blame him if he finally succumbed?

"All right," he said. "Let's go."

The cloakroom would serve nicely, he thought. The only trick would be sneaking past the chaperones.

To the Dean Reverend he said: "There's a fellow getting sick in the lav. I believe he's intoxicated."

To Mrs. Vanderlip he said: "There's a girl behind the stage pulling the hem off her dress. Her knees— Oh, my! It's shocking! Horrible! I believe I shall faint!"

When the coast was clear, MacInnes and Marjorie darted down a hall lined with portraits of dead benefactors. They slipped inside the cloakroom and were taken aback when a voice from the shadows said: "Find your own petting parlor, chum. This one's taken."

MacInnes bristled. What now? If the authorities spotted them together like this, alone in the hall, they'd be beaten for sure. He should never have— Wait. He had it.

"Let's go," he said. "And give me a hairpin."

He led her to the pantry, neatly picked the lock, and found a cozy spot between two crates of National Biscuits.

She tasted as luscious as he'd hoped. They petted until it became imperative that he adjust the front of his trousers.

"Gosh," she said. "I feel all tingly."

"Yeah," he managed to say.

"I meant the music! Don't you love jazz?"

"Oh. Sure."

"It's the rhythm! The pounding! It goes straight to my body. Everything they say about it is true. Those primitive tribes know how to live, I tell you."

MacInnes was about to show her that he also knew how to live when she quickly changed the subject.

"Hey, you don't have any cigarettes? I absolutely adore them, but we're not allowed to smoke. One little puff, and it's bye-bye, Marj. It happened to my roommate last year. Mrs. Vanderlip sniffs out the nicotine on our fingertips."

MacInnes took a crumpled pack of Fatimas from his pocket.

"How're you going to smoke, then?"

She explained a little trick that some of the girls had told her about. MacInnes lit a cigarette, puffed without inhaling, and blew a stream of smoke into her mouth. Marjorie sucked it down as if stealing his life-wind. Even in the darkness, her eyes glowed with it. She coughed a little, but that was all right.

"Sorry," she said. "It's just been ages since I smoked!"

MacInnes was sure he would explode. He pressed his mouth over hers and felt a grain of tobacco on her tongue, tasted the bite of the smoke—and then his hand was on her breast, her buttons seemed to unfasten themselves, his trousers more uncomfortable than ever, a spark of salt on his lips—and then he was gathering folds of her dress in his hands, furling it up, wanting her now, sure it would happen, the curve of her hip—then his fingertips ever so gently finding their way beneath a layer of silk, and then—

CRASH!

—he was rubbing the side of his face.

"Hey!" he cried. "What's the big idea?"

"That's what I wanna know!" Already fastening her buttons.

"Well—" MacInnes was shocked.

"What kind of girl do you take me for?"

"But it was you who asked me," he protested.

"Look here, buster. Just because a girl likes to pet doesn't mean she's immoral. I come from good people."

"Well, you don't have to be sore about it."

"Who're you calling sore? I'm not sore."

In fact, she was all smiles. MacInnes, on the other hand, was not. It wasn't that she'd left him hanging—lots of girls had done that before. But her emotions were too well timed. Her lines were too practiced. She'd played this game before, and he didn't like being her patsy.

"We'd better get back," he grumbled.

Ditching her, unfortunately, turned out to be impossible. He was too much of a gentleman to tell her to get lost, and anything short of that flew right past her.

"It's been very nice meeting you," he tried.

"Same here, handsome. Let's grab something to eat."

And so they were at the buffet when he finally saw Laura. She was standing alone—unconsciously beautiful in a simple dress—and he knew at once he was smitten.

"Is that Laura Waverly?"

"Sure enough," Marjorie said. "Do you know her?"

"We met a long time ago. What's she like?"

"She's the biggest snob I know."

MacInnes almost choked on his punch.

"Really?"

"Absolutely. She has almost no friends at all."

"And that makes her a snob?"

"Of course." Marjorie smiled cunningly and added, "Do you wanna dance with her? I'll walk you over."

"Why would you want to do that?"

"I don't know much about you, handsome, but I do know this: Laura Waverly is out of your reach. And that makes her no threat to my interest whatsoever."

"How do you figure that?"

"She's rich. You're not."

"You seem pretty sure of yourself."

"Believe me, I know."

She led him firmly by the hand.

"Oh, Laura?" she said. "I've met someone who claims to be an acquaintance of yours."

Laura's eyes met his, and she smiled.

"I wondered if you were here," she said.

"I've been wondering the same thing."

She sighed. "Trent's been hiding me in the corner. He worries that if he lets me out of his sight I'll vanish forever."

"He hasn't—uh—"

She shook her head. "He's been perfectly charming. You and the Dean Reverend seem to have straightened him out."

"Well—good."

She smiled again. "You're wearing the jacket. I'm flattered."

He didn't know how to answer that, so he asked her to dance.

"I shouldn't."

"But you will?"

"All right."

They walked closer to the orchestra, and he started laughing.

"What is it?" Laura said.

"I don't actually know how to dance."

"Are you serious?"

"A tragic flaw in my upbringing."

"I'll teach you, then. Put your hand here—"

"Like this?"

"Perfect. Now, they're playing a waltz. That means there are three beats to every measure—"

They started moving in circles.

"ONE two three, ONE two three, FEEL the beat, THAT's the way. Are you sure you've never done this before?"

"On my honor. Why?"

"Because you've already got the hang of it. I'm amazed."

A comically matched twosome—she was tall, he was short—were galloping toward them, awkward as mules. MacInnes steered Laura in another direction and deftly avoided the crash.

"Is it supposed to be hard?" he asked.

"I took lessons for years."

"Well, there you are. You've passed your expertise on to me."

"But I've hardly—"

The lights went out. Near darkness enveloped the ballroom. The orchestra stopped playing, and the dancers groaned.

MacInnes instinctively pulled Laura close to him. She slipped into his arms, and it was as if he'd discovered a missing piece of himself. Something more deeply interfused . . .

"Who are you?" she whispered. "I mean, who are you really?"

"I think you already know."

She laughed nervously. "Tell me anyway."

"You and I have been lovers since before the dawn of time."

Her eyes widened—but before she could say another word, the lights came back on, and they slipped out of each other's grasp.

"Oh, *here* you are, darling."

Bloxom. Zounds! He stepped between them and clapped a hand on Laura's shoulder. The gesture's meaning was clear: "She's mine."

"I turn my back for five minutes, and—" Bloxom narrowed his eyes. "MacInnes! I should've known you were behind this."

"Behind what, old chum?"

"Trying to steal my girl!"

"She's not a heifer, you dolt. She goes where she chooses."

"Trent," Laura said, "we were only dancing."

"Is that right, MacInnes? Dancing?"

"Sure."

"Well—" Bloxom seemed to be struggling for the appropriate words. "Don't forget I owe you a good punch in the nose."

And with that, he whisked her away. She glanced back with an apologetic look on her face, but all MacInnes cared about was that she was leaving. There'd been so much more he'd wanted to say, so many questions he'd wanted to ask. And now she was gone.

Marjorie was dumbfounded.

"That was the strangest thing I've seen in my life. Just how well *do* you know Laura?"

"Not very."

"Well, you could've fooled me. The way you were dancing, I thought you'd been partners for years. Other people saw it too. They were *staring*."

"Really?" He liked the idea.

"And when Trent showed up—golly, the look on his face."

"Pretty mad, eh?"

"Worried, you mean. What were you and Laura talking about?"

"The usual stuff. Just catching up."

"All right, don't tell me. It doesn't matter. She's still out of your reach."

The orchestra played a final song and then packed up their instruments. The Grand Cotillion was over.

"Oh, girls!" Mrs. Vanderlip called. "Time to say goodbye!"

"Oh, pooh," Marjorie said. "Let's write each other, okay? Or better yet, phone me. We could arrange a tryst or a rendezvous or whatever it is that couples arrange."

"Couples!" MacInnes barked.

"Why, of course we're a couple, silly. You don't think I pet with just anyone?"

She kissed him smack on the mouth. It was a teasing sort of kiss—the kind that promised better things to come—and he felt like her patsy all over again.

"So long, handsome."

"Yeah. I'll see ya."

Student volunteers were already taking down the decorations. MacInnes didn't feel like leaving yet, so he wandered over to the ice sculptures—what remained of them anyway. Broken walls and columns floated in a pool of water. He wondered which tiny window was Laura's. He wondered if he would see her again, or if—in this world of waltzes and tuxedos—Marjorie was all he could hope for.

"Good night, Michael MacInnes," a familiar voice said.

He looked up just as someone in a large orange turban walked out the front door. Miss Dubois! He was sure of it! But what was *she* doing here? He didn't want to lose track of her again, so he leapt through an open window.

"Hey!" someone said. "You can't—"

He landed in the bushes. Taking care not to ruin his jacket, he stood up and looked around. Miss Dubois ought to have been in plain sight, but he couldn't see her anywhere.

He stopped a fellow on the sidewalk.

"Did you see a woman out here?"

"Sure, pal," the boy said drunkenly. "Lots of 'em. In case you didn't notice, we just had a dance."

"No, no, I mean an *older* woman."

"You say you're looking for an old lady?"

"That's right."

"It's disgusting, is what it is."

"Oh, you misunderstand," MacInnes said, and walked off.

"Hey, Buchanan!" the fellow called. "Guy here says he likes . . . Well, he was here a minute ago. Say! How'd you like that cutie in the hat?"

15

Alas, alas, who's injured by my love?
—JOHN DONNE

An eternity later, MacInnes crept into the tower. All the gas jets were off, and the room was a confusion of shadows—some trousers here, a pile of books there. A scrap of moonlight fell through the window and lit up Roger's bed—where Roger and Daphne lay sleeping in each other's arms.

"It's about time," MacInnes muttered.

He went out to the widow's walk and smoked for a while. He would write her a poem—kill Bloxom—kill himself . . .

There was a rustle beside him, and Roger sat down.

"How was the dance?"

"Don't ask."

"That bad?"

"For five minutes it was wonderful. I can't bring myself to talk about the rest of it, chum. Tell me about your evening."

Roger described the search for Entwistle's stash.

"I really thought we had it," he said. "And then, nothing."

MacInnes tossed a cigarette butt into the rain trough. It was a clear night, and they sat quietly for a while, each one absorbed by his own thoughts. Eventually, Roger mumbled something.

"How's that?" MacInnes said.

"I said you're probably waiting for an explanation."

"About what?"

"Well—about my being—about Daphne—and me—"

"Oh, *that*," MacInnes said. "I've known about that for weeks."

"But you couldn't have! Tonight was the first time."

"Sure, but I could tell something was developing."

Roger snorted. "And here I was keeping it a secret."

"You can't hide who you are. Not for long anyway."

"I suppose you'll want a new roommate."

"Rubbish," MacInnes said. "If we're going to be chums, you'll have to give me more credit than that."

"You mean it?"

"As far as I'm concerned, nothing's changed."

"Well—thanks." The relief in Roger's voice was enormous.

"I do have one question," MacInnes said.

"Ask away."

"Well, I'm reluctant to bring it up. You might think I'm conceited or something."

"Conceited? You?"

"I just wondered . . . why you've never been attracted to *me*."

Roger laughed, and MacInnes felt himself blushing.

"It's not that ridiculous," he grumbled.

"Of course it is," Roger said. "I've never met anyone who was so perfectly adapted to the opposite sex. You'd make a lousy homosexual."

MacInnes thought it over.

"Yes," he said finally. "I suppose you're right. And you haven't even heard about Marjorie yet . . ."

16

Such gaudy tulips raised from dung . . .
—JONATHAN SWIFT

By midafternoon MacInnes could take it no longer. He went down to the Craxton House parlor and chased a freshman off the telephone. He'd never actually used a telephone before (he had of course seen them used on many occasions), and he had some trouble mastering the switch hook. But after a few dozen clicks he managed to establish a connection without cutting it off right away.

"Thank you," a woman's voice said. "Number, please."

"HULLO, OPERATOR?"

"There's no need to shout, sir."

"WHAT?"

"I can hear you just fine, sir."

"Oh." Godforsaken contraptions. "Sorry."

"What number would you like, sir?"

"Ah—the Hood School."

"Thank you, sir. Which extension?"

"I don't know—which do you recommend?"

"What's the name of your party, sir?"

"I'm afraid that's strictly confidential."

A long pause ensued.

"Sir, I can't connect you without a name or a number."

"Oh. Yes, I see your point." It was a dilemma, all right. He should have seen this coming. "Very well, operator. I'm calling a student. Her name is—"

"I'll connect you to the dormitory, sir."

MacInnes wiped the sweat off his forehead. The world was mad, and he was the only one who knew it. He envisioned a future where people lived in Bakelite jars and communicated only by telephone. No more need for love or sex—just *phone* it in. Eventually, people would be born with telephone wires embedded in their brains. Just think of all the time and anguish they'd save when they never had to meet face-to-face. Just think of all the—

"Hullo?" It was a girl's voice this time.

"Hullo, is this the Hood School dormitory?"

"It might be." Muffled giggling in the background.

"I'm trying to reach Laura Waverly. Is she there?"

The giggles turned to oohs and aahs.

"Whom shall I say is calling?"

He told her.

"I see. And does she know you, Mr. MacInnes?"

"Not very well, I'm afraid."

"Then I shouldn't get my hopes up if I were you."

There was a scrape and a bump, and he was afraid for a moment they'd been disconnected. Then he noticed the twinkling of a piano and a good deal of whispering and giggling. He wondered idly if it was true that girls who lived in dormitories all shared the same menstrual cycle. If it *was* true, it was the most idiotic plan he'd ever heard of.

There was another scrape, and then the sound of moist lips.

"Michael MacInnes!" a voice said. "As I live and breathe!"

It was all he could do not to swoon.

"Marjorie—?"

"Were you expecting someone else?"

"Well, no. Of course not."

"When I heard Doris mention your name in the hall, I thought I would just up and die! Would you believe I spent the whole night thinking I'd made a damned fool of myself— and here you spent the whole night thinking of *me*."

"That's true," he lied.

"You are *so* sweet!"

"Well . . ."

"I suppose you'd like to meet me someplace."

"The thought did cross my mind."

What? Who said that?

"Let's meet at the old barn," she said. "Give me an hour."

"Where's the old barn?" he started to ask, but she'd already broken the connection.

His worst fears were coming true. He would never be allowed to see Laura. He was destined to be with Marjorie. He was in the hands of some terrible cosmic force.

Well—might as well make the best of it.

He remembered an abandoned hayloft a few miles down the road. No doubt this was the "old barn." He hoped so anyway. It was the perfect spot for lovers.

It was raining, so he borrowed Roger's raincoat.

The road to the barn was a wasteland of mud-filled ruts that nearly sucked the shoes off his feet. It was not a well-traveled road, and the one time he tried waving down a car for a lift, the driver squeezed his horn and ran him into the drainage gully.

He scrambled back to the road and hurled a rock at the car.

"Come back here, you coward!"

If he'd been uncertain about seeing Marjorie before, he was determined to see her now. He was a knight on a romantic quest. He was Lancelot—Ivanhoe—off to rescue the princess from cutthroats and infidels and inconsiderate drivers.

"I'm coming, Marjorie!" he cried through the downpour.

By now, the rain was crashing around him. He could barely see through the foam that clung to his lashes. His shoes were so heavy with clay that every step was an effort. Still, he pressed onward. He thought of Marjorie's lips, and the warmth of her taut southern body. What more inspiration did he need? Laura Waverly was a dream—a fantasy. Marjorie was real. And she wanted him.

"I'm coming!" he cried again.

At last he staggered into the hayloft.

"Marjorie?"

No answer.

"Is anyone here?"

He shrugged. He found a woodstove and kindled a fire, then laid his wet clothes out to dry. Twenty minutes later he put them back on. Marjorie had not yet arrived. Had she turned back in the rain? Was her devotion to him as fragile as that?

"All right," a voice said. "Just turn around real slow-like."

MacInnes did as he was told.

An ancient farmer had sneaked up behind him with a pitchfork.

"What's yer name?"

MacInnes told him.

"You one of them Academy boys?"

"Yes, sir."

"I only ask because you don't look stupid. Most Academy boys look stupid to me. You look like you've been around the block a time or two. Makes me wonder about yer intentions."

MacInnes decided to play it honest. "I'm meeting a girl."

"Here?"

"I thought so. Isn't this the old barn?"

It was a full minute before the farmer stopped laughing.

"I guess you ain't as clever as I took you for!"

"What do you mean?"

The farmer leaned his pitchfork against a timber post. "My truck's outside. Start her up, and I'll show you."

The truck was started by a crank. MacInnes gripped the handle and turned it for all he was worth. Nothing happened. He tried this two more times before the farmer called, "Use the choke! Use the choke!"

MacInnes must have looked confused, because the farmer came around and pointed to a loop of wire. MacInnes tugged it gently and tried the crank again. The engine started. He hopped inside, and they splashed off through the rain.

Soon they rattled up to the Stoney Batter Inn, a fixture on Main Street in town. MacInnes could not help noticing the gambrel roof and wrought-iron hardware that he'd seen, but not considered, before.

"*This* is the old barn?"

"That's what the kids call it—all except you!"

MacInnes shook his hand. "Thanks for the lift."

The farmer winked. "Give that girl of yours a kiss for me!"

He found Marjorie and a tribe of girlfriends at a dark, smoky table in the restaurant's farthest corner. They looked like a page out of *Vanity Fair*, with their cloche hats, feathers, strings of beads, and flapping galoshes. A taste like burnt cabbage rose into his mouth. Somehow he'd gotten the impression that Marjorie was above all that nonsense. Or maybe he'd just hoped she was.

"Oh, my," she said now. "Look what the cat dragged in."

"Forgive me," he said. "It was a terrible mix-up."

"We're all *dying* to hear what happened."

"I have no excuse," he said, "apart from being an idiot."

Marjorie sighed and seemed to think this over. "I'll have to speak with my colleagues."

The four young ladies huddled together and spoke in accusing whispers. One of them had a habit of looking his way and clucking her tongue in disapproval. Eventually they announced a deadlock and asked if he'd brought any tobacco.

"Won't Mrs. Vanderlip be suspicious?"

"What makes you say that?"

He shrugged. No matter. He was in.

Marjorie made introductions while the girls fitted cigarettes into enormous holders. Fern was from Wilmington, where her family owned a chemical plant. Nell was from Philadelphia. Her family made textiles. Eddie was from Chicago, and her family owned bonds. ("Her real name is Edwina. Can you imagine?") All four had come to the Hood

School to prep for colleges like Vassar and Smith. ("What *they* shall prep us for is anyone's guess.")

"Michael," Marjorie said, "is from Baltimore."

"Oh?" Fern arched an eyebrow. "What do your people do?"

By now, MacInnes loathed them, so he allowed his mischievous streak to run wild.

"I come from a long line of professional soldiers," he said. "Primarily in the Espionage Corps. Spies, saboteurs—that sort of thing."

"Really!"

"How exciting!"

"Tragically, my father was killed in the War."

"Oh, how awful!"

"Yes," he agreed. "He was mining an enemy harbor when one of the bombs simply exploded. They buried what was left of him in the Argonne Forest. I take a lot of satisfaction knowing that there's a corner of some foreign field that is forever America." He waved his arm to suggest the breadth of his vision.

Nell was moved to tears. "That is *so* beautiful!"

Edwina was more critical: "Why'd they bury him in the forest if he died in the harbor?"

"Sentiment," he said quickly. "We're a sentimental family."

"Ah."

"Was it just you and your mother then?"

"No. I never knew my mother. She died in childbirth. After my father died, I was raised by my grandfather—when he wasn't doing secret work for the army, that is."

"Why, you poor thing!" Marjorie said. "I had no idea!"

"I usually keep it to myself."

"Will you follow in your father's footsteps?" Nell asked.

He nodded thoughtfully. "If my country needs me, I shall make the ultimate sacrifice, of course. Otherwise, I consider it my duty to enjoy the fruits of peace."

They raised glasses of Coke and drank to the fruits of peace.

"What will you do for a living?" Fern asked.

"I think I shall be a poet."

"Well, isn't that a coincidence!" Edwina said. "Did you tell him what your family does, Marj?"

"They own a few magazines," Marjorie said lightly.

"Librarians, are they?"

"Don't be silly, handsome. They *publish* the magazines."

MacInnes felt the blood drain from his face.

"Er"—trying not to choke—"which magazines, darling?"

She rattled off a list of names. He lit a cigarette from the one burning in his hand and tried to steady himself.

"Most of those have poetry sections," he remarked.

"Do they?" Marjorie said. "I never noticed."

"You never noticed the most avant-garde poetry in America?"

"I stick mainly to the fashions."

"Oh."

Fern was tapping her watch. "It's time to go, ladies."

After a flurry of coats and umbrellas, MacInnes and Marjorie found themselves alone for a discreet thirty seconds. He kissed her politely—and when their lips parted, he noticed a fire in her eyes that had not been there at the dance. Had something changed? Had he passed some sort of test?

"I want to see you again," she said. "Just the two of us."

"I want to see you too. I want to ask you about—"

"Come on, Marjorie!" Fern called from the door.

He mumbled something about writing a letter. She kissed his cheek and was gone.

On his way to the restaurant lav, he was met by a waiter who handed him a note "from the young lady." He put it in his pocket and didn't dare read it until he was halfway back to campus. It was written on exquisite paper, and he stared in amazement until the rain had washed away its simple message:

Sorry I missed your call. Meet me at the shooting range. Wednesday—4 p.m. Laura

"Oh, no!" he cried. "What the hell am I supposed to do now?"

17

Pity in a man of knowledge seems almost ludicrous.
—FRIEDRICH NIETZSCHE

Howard Entwistle left the infirmary. His bowels had been flushed, his pimples drained, and both his cheeks painted with a mixture of cornstarch and camphor. It was an ugly concoction that had to stay on his face for hours—and while he waited, he preferred not to be seen by acquaintances.

He popped open his umbrella and walked to the village park. It was an absurd place, decorated with footbridges and maypoles, and it always reminded him of baseball and tubas. Its one saving grace was an eight-sided pavilion, and it was here that he sat, protected from the elements, on a sagging wooden bench.

On his way to breakfast this morning, Entwistle had spotted a trash can filled with broken glass—at least two dozen smashed-up bottles. Their labels had all been carefully removed, but he knew what they were, and he knew they were his. The missing cases of whiskey. Someone had entered his room last night and stolen them.

At first, he'd been too enraged to think.

But now, tranquilized by the patter of rain on the pavilion, he knew who the guilty parties must be.

MacInnes. Legrande. Daphne.

Fortunately, they had not found the stash. Fools! Simpletons! Had they really believed that Howard Entwistle's supply consisted of a mere two cases of whiskey?

A small boy ran into the pavilion. He was soaked to the skin and shivering. Entwistle smiled.

"Hello, little boy," he said.

"Hello," said the boy. "Have you seen my string?"

"Your string?"

"I lost it here yesterday. Do you have it?"

"Hmm," said Entwistle. "Now that you mention it, I think I did see some string. Come sit next to me while I remember."

The boy wrapped his arms around his chest and frowned.

"Don't be afraid," Entwistle said.

"I ain't," said the boy.

"Of course you're not! You're a very brave little boy."

"I ain't little either."

"Did I say little? I meant big. You're a big, brave boy."

The boy nodded and sat on the bench next to Entwistle's.

"What's on your face?" he said.

"Why, it's paint of course."

"Like a clown?"

"Exactly like a clown. Clowns wear masks, don't they?"

"Yup."

"Do you know why they wear masks?"

The boy shook his head.

"It's to hide what's underneath," Entwistle whispered. "Do you know what a *skull* is, little boy?"

The boy's eyes got big and round. He nodded.

"Of course you do. It's the bone that lies under a person's face, isn't it? Usually, you don't see a skull unless someone's been dead for a very long time. The face keeps it hidden. But we clowns don't have faces. That's why we wear painted masks. It's to hide our skulls."

Entwistle grinned. The little boy squirmed.

"Would you like to see my skull, little boy?"

"Nooo . . ."

"Ah, but you shall. Watch closely. I have some buttons in the back of my head, and when I unfasten the buttons—"

"No!" The boy leapt to his feet and ran out of the pavilion. He shot through the grass crying, "No! No! No!"

Entwistle laughed maniacally.

Five minutes later, the boy returned to the park with a man who was no doubt his father. Even from a distance, his arms looked as meaty as hams. Entwistle had made a mistake. His heart skipped a beat. When the man started walking toward the pavilion, Entwistle jumped to his feet and walked in the other direction.

He looked over his shoulder. The man was still coming.

"Hey, you!" he called. "That's right, fatso, you."

Entwistle ran. He didn't run well, but he had a head start. He ran to the creek and followed it away from the park. It flowed through a part of town he had not known existed: smoky shacks built of unpainted boards, sheep and pigs wallowing in their own steamy waste, rusted plow blades, heaps of trash.

He stopped. He was winded. His umbrella was in tatters. His facial ointment dripped off his chin. He risked a look behind him.

The man was gone.

Entwistle squatted on the bank of the creek for a long, long time. His chest heaved up and down. Eventually he stood, discarded the umbrella, and splashed through someone's yard. When he came to the street, he realized he was lost. East side, west side—nothing looked familiar. He walked for a block and hoped he would come to a landmark. He didn't.

"Holy Jesus!" a voice cried. "What happened to you?"

He looked up. He was standing in front of a shabby house. On the porch stood a woman. She was in her forties, he supposed, and wore only a nightdress. He found it most unsavory.

"I beg your pardon?"

"I don't know you," she mused. "Have you been here before?"

"Madam, I don't even know where 'here' is."

"Tell you what. I'll let you have a round for half price."

"Excuse me?"

"You want a girl, don't you?"

"A girl?" He was dumbfounded. "What do you mean?"

"There's no need to be shy, sweetie."

The truth struck him all at once. This house was a brothel. She was asking if he wanted to exchange money for sex.

Frankly, he was curious. He'd never been with a girl, and it might be just the thing to cheer him up.

She led him into a dingy parlor that reeked of sour beer and stale tobacco. The chairs were adorned with antimacassars, and the ceiling was smudged with soot.

"How can we help you?" she said.

Entwistle blinked, suddenly realizing he hadn't a clue what to ask for.

"Er—what would you suggest?"

"For a sophisticated gentleman like yourself? I'd recommend Genevieve."

"Genevieve," he echoed.

"She's very French and very gentle."

"She sounds . . . very nice."

"That'll be ten dollars in advance."

Was it a reasonable fee? He had nothing to compare it with. He found his billfold and produced the required sum. The proprietress concealed it among the folds of her dress and whisked him upstairs. All but one of the doors off the hall were closed, and as they passed the open one, he saw bath towels, a toilet, a claw-footed tub. The house was not simply a business—it was someone's home. The thought depressed him beyond words.

"Just give me a moment," the proprietress said.

While she was gone, he cleaned his face and combed his hair. His fantasies ran wild. Genevieve would turn out to be a Parisian prima donna (recently retired). A Negress. A transvestite. An heiress to the Russian throne. In one look, they would fall in love. He would teach her about the great philosophers, and she would teach him . . . other things.

"Genevieve will entertain you now," the proprietress said as she swept open a door at the end of the hall.

He nodded politely and stepped inside.

The bedroom was as cramped and dingy as the parlor. On the edge of a mattress—there was no bed—sat a girl who was not much older than Entwistle. She wore the V-shaped undergarments he'd noticed in many of the photos he sold, but her pose lacked their whimsy and coquettishness. (Indeed, she looked like nothing so much as someone's little sister.)

"Hi there," she said through a yawn.

"Good morning. You must be Genevieve."

"Is that what Prue called me?"

Her name, she explained, was Jenny. She wasn't French but had once lived near the Canadian border, and this fact had made an impression on the proprietress. Entwistle tried to hide his disappointment.

"So," she said. "What's it going to be?"

"Er—the usual."

He stood foolishly in front of the mattress and was grateful when she instructed him to remove his clothes. He began to do so, and was disappointed all over again when he saw there was no place to put them. He put his shoes on the floor and built a soggy little tower, all the while conscious of her eyes upon his body.

"I guess you go to the Academy," she remarked.

"What makes you say that?"

"You talk kinda fancy."

"Ah."

"I never liked school," she added. "It always seemed dumb."

Under different circumstances, he would have responded with any of a dozen cutting remarks—but he elected to say nothing. He was too far out of his element.

"Hey," she said. "Don't you want to take off your undies?"

"Is that customary?"

"Only if you want what you paid for."

He stripped off the last sure barrier between himself and

the world. This was apparently a signal for her to remove her own small clothes, and he just caught a glimpse of her tea-brown nipples before heaving himself under the blankets.

"Whoa!" she exclaimed. "Are you cold or something, mister?"

"Jenny, you have no idea."

What followed was an exercise in futility. The humiliations of his youth were meager in comparison. After a while, he simply gave up. He rolled onto his side and studied the peeling wallpaper.

"Aw, come on," she said. "You're just nervous, is all."

"Leave me alone."

"Maybe you could—you know—get it started by yourself."

"That's disgusting."

"No, it's not. Lotsa guys—"

"Be quiet."

"What're you getting sore at me for? Haven't I been—"

"I told you to be quiet."

"Hey." She sat up. "I don't have to take that crap."

"Certainly you do. I paid in advance."

"Not for this you didn't. We have our standards."

"Standards!"

"Listen. You might not think so, but I've been pretty damned nice. It's Saturday, you know? I was doing you a favor because Prue said you were a wreck. And this is your way of saying thanks? Get the hell out of here."

"You bitch," he muttered. "I could *own* you. I could own this whole house."

"Think again, charlie."

She was suddenly holding a revolver. He looked down its black maw and made a fast decision. He flung out his hand and snatched the gun away. It was heavier than he'd expected, and for some reason this filled him with joy.

"Now this," he said, "is an interesting reversal of fortune. Don't you agree?"

"Jesus Christ! You're crazy, you know that?"

"It has occurred to me, yes. Now be a good girl and sit very still."

"I ain't moving a muscle."

He dressed efficiently and went downstairs. He left the brothel without another word to anyone. The revolver was in his pocket.

Crazy indeed.

18

I have a great mind to believe in Christianity for the mere pleasure of fancying I may be damned.
—GEORGE GORDON, LORD BYRON

After dinner, MacInnes and Roger played chess in the tower. Roger played carefully, maneuvering his pieces into classical positions, taking no risks, awaiting the endgame. MacInnes, meanwhile, played with reckless abandon, making suicide attacks on Roger's formations, leaving his king undefended, and usually—to Roger's amazement—winning decisively. It was the same style he used when running his life. Or so Roger thought.

"Don't you get it?" MacInnes was saying. "I can't pretend to love Marjorie just because her father might publish my stuff. It wouldn't be honest."

"Honest?" Roger said. "You stole the Dean Reverend's car!"

"We gave it back in one piece, didn't we?"

"I suppose. What about your smoking, then?"

"Now you're being silly, chum. That's just rules for the sake of rules. I'm talking about honesty in a cosmic sense."

"I thought you were an atheist."

"I still believe in *something*."

Roger toyed with a pawn. "So what's this plan you mentioned?"

"Do you remember a conversation we had about publishing my own magazine?"

"I ought to remember. It was my idea."

MacInnes twitched his eyebrows.

"You mean you want to do it *now*?" Roger said.

"Oh, no, not now. Now would be very bad timing. Now is out."

"That's a relief."

"I thought we'd do it later tonight."

Roger shook his head. "So much for my calculus test."

"You'll help me, then?"

"Of course I will. I promised, didn't I?"

"See that? Cosmic honesty."

"More like cosmic lunacy."

"Oh, and one more thing, chum."

"What's that?"

MacInnes moved his queen across the board. "Checkmate."

Sometime between midnight and breakfast, a crudely set folio was slid beneath every door and pinned to every bulletin board on campus. Printed front and back, for a grand total of four pages, it contained a half dozen poems and an apocalyptic essay on "the poetic sensibility." Its author: unknown. Its name: *The Heretic*.

By breakfast, it was the topic of everyone's conversation.

"Who is the Heretic?"

"Why all the secrecy?"

"What does he want?"

The poems were obscure enough that no one understood them.

"What the devil is a 'swollen thunderhead'?"

"Or a 'savage garden-belly moist untrue'?"

"Is *satiety* a real word? I can't even pronounce it."

The essay, on the other hand, aroused quite a stir, with its emphasis on freedom in place of rules, intuition instead of fact, sexuality for the sake of enlightenment, and a variety of remarks that bordered on blasphemy.

The true poet [the Heretic had written] does not trust a God who seems not to trust him. If man is a cosmos, and beauty is truth, and love is all—there is no point in asking, "Do I dare?" For God's sake, hold your tongue and let me love. Bite the apple and let the juices roll off your chin. The true poet is a farmer-priest. He worships the world as he worships his own passion.

"Yeah," someone remarked. "But what does it mean?"

By midmorning, rumors abounded. The Heretic was an atheist, a Catholic, a Jew. A malcontented master. The Dean Reverend gone mad. A prophet, a devil, a homosexual, a socialist.

At one point, Charlie Schlage was seen in the quad with at least a hundred copies of the magazine and was consequently tackled by the football team, who were sure they had their man. It turned out he was only collecting them in hopes of somehow earning a percentage.

At least two dozen fistfights broke out in the halls, and Dr. Cornwell's medical log would later indicate that he sutured three head wounds and set two broken fingers.

Such was "Heretic Madness."

By noon prayer, a new rumor was forming on everyone's lips: that Trent Bloxom knew the identity of the Heretic and was prepared to denounce him at lunch. The meal was eaten in record time as the entire community—students and masters—awaited the revelation. When all the dishes had been cleared, the Dean Reverend reminded everyone that dirty bedsheets should be exchanged for clean ones at the campus laundry. Coach Curran announced that there would be a freshman scrimmage on Bugg's Field. When Bloxom approached the lectern, the dining hall went silent.

"The Heretic," he said, "is Michael MacInnes."

"Proof!" someone cried. "Where's your proof?"

Bloxom thrust a leather satchel over his head. "MacInnes has been submitting material to *The Stoney Batter Review* all semester. Many of these items—which I hesitate to call poetry—appear in *The Heretic*. The facts speak for themselves."

"What about it, Muh-ginnis?" Nathaniel Beauregard drawled.

"Out with it!"

"Out with it!"

"Out with it!"

The primitive chant, accompanied by the stomping of feet on the floor and the pounding of hands on tables, was deafening. The masters looked at one another in terror. Who knew what the mob might do?

Eventually, MacInnes stood on a chair and waved them silent.

"It's true," he confessed. "I am the Heretic."

The room seemed to explode. Half the crowd cheered—they were mostly Craxton House boys. The other half called for his head.

The Dean Reverend dismissed lunch by clearing the phlegm from his throat, and that was the official Stoney Batter response.

For now, at least.

Entwistle confronted MacInnes in the foyer. "Congratulations," he said. "You really have them fooled."

"You wouldn't know a piece of literature if it bit you on the ass."

"Wouldn't I?" Entwistle chuckled. "Don't be so sure."

Mr. Moffett was cautiously supportive. "I see you took matters into your own hands, eh?"

"How do you like it?"

"It's great. Really avant-garde stuff. Right on the edge."

"But—?"

"You're taking an awful chance. You can only push the Dean Reverend so far. You really ought to be careful."

Mr. Hamilton-Smythe simply liked the principle of the thing. "I haven't actually found time to read it," he said. "But I am impressed with the response! We haven't had a phenomenon like this in a long time—not since Jiggers O'Brien climbed the chapel steeple back in 1904. I feel twenty years younger."

"I really didn't expect—"

"Nonsense! I recognized a spark in you the day we first met. You're a genuine character. That's why I asked you to represent Craxton in the Quintilian Oratory. Speaking of which, I want you to reserve some of this talent for your speech. It's just a few weeks away, you know."

MacInnes had forgotten. "Oh, yes," he said. "I'm just giving it a final polish."

"Splendid! If it's as popular as your magazine, we're sure to take home the laurels."

"I'll do my best."

"I hope so." He put his mouth to MacInnes's ear. "Tell me the truth: how did you manage to get the thing printed?"

"You promise not to peach?"

"When have I ever?"

"Roger and I broke into the *Review* and used their equipment."

"Hah! You're a character, my boy. A genuine character!"

MacInnes spent the rest of the afternoon writing autographs and ignoring dirty looks.

Another edition of *The Heretic* appeared Tuesday morning. This one was frankly sexual and unapologetically atheist.

My love commands
the ocean of my lust
the tidal pool

the surging wave
the warm salt spray

Einstein cracked the atomic acorn, searching for that old whore God. What did he find instead? Vapor and speculation and an empty valise on the nightstand.

The reaction was predictable.

"There are some among us," the Dean Reverend said at morning prayer, "who insist that God is a myth. I say to you now, this is false prophecy. To give it a morsel of credence is to risk eternal damnation. As the Good Book teaches, the heavens will tremble, and the earth will be shaken. Jesus wept for your sins. Jesus bled for your sins. Believe in Jesus, and you will be saved . . ."

After dinner, Trent Bloxom lit a fire in the quad and burned every copy of *The Heretic* he could find. He was not alone. Dozens of boys added their copies too. A handful of zealots even raided the library for works by Shakespeare, Byron, Shelley, and Darwin. The flames rose higher. A ribbon of smoke curled into the sky.

"Religion," the Heretic had written, "abhors free thought."

Roger found MacInnes reading Milton's *Areopagitica* in the tower.

"The Dean Reverend wants to see you," he said.

"I wondered when he'd get round to it."

Roger said nothing.

MacInnes opened a window and lit a cigarette. "Yesterday I was a hero. They all lined up to shake my hand."

"They're stupid bastards. You know that."

"This is supposed to be a place of learning, for God's sake. What's the point if we can't speak our minds?"

Roger shook his head. "I don't know."

MacInnes found Mr. Moffett's cottage amid a copse of black trees. The master came to the door and ushered him inside.

"You look terrible," he said.

"The bastard's going to throw me out!"

"I warned you not to push him."

"What am I going to do?"

"Do you have much choice?"

"I thought *you* might speak to him."

Mr. Moffett was drinking coffee. He looked into his cup as if he were ashamed to meet MacInnes's eyes.

"Look," he said. "I admire what you're doing. Some of this is really fine stuff. Even better than yesterday's."

"But—?"

"I'm up for tenure next year. I don't dare put my neck out."

MacInnes nodded glumly. "I understand."

"If it were anything else . . ."

"No. It's all right."

"I really am sorry."

He had better luck with Mr. Hamilton-Smythe. Apparently there was something to be said for all that age and experience stuff.

"Leave everything to me," the old fellow said.

When he returned from Roderick Hall, he was smiling. "Good news, MacInnes! You shan't be expelled!"

"Thank you." He thought for a moment. "And *The Heretic*?"

"Oh, dear boy, that's done for. I thought you realized."

"You mean he wants me to change it?"

"I mean it's dead. One more edition, under that or any other name, and you *will* be expelled. He made that very clear."

MacInnes was outraged. "This is a damned injustice!"

"Get used to it, my boy."

"Do you think it's right?"

"No. But I don't make the rules. People like you and me never do. The best we can hope for is not to get caught in their infernal machinery."

"What kind of life is that?"

"A long one, I hope. Now, go see the Dean Reverend."

"But I thought—"

"I'm afraid some things are beyond even my help."

MacInnes was a few seconds catching his drift. "Oh."

"It's the Stoney Batter way, my boy. You can't fight it."

"Perhaps you think I'm a monster—that I enjoy punishing boys who stray close to the vortex. Let me assure you it's a necessary evil."

MacInnes had to admit the Dean Reverend looked terrifying behind that big desk—and the large blue vein that pulsed in his forehead did nothing to change the impression. He hoped the fear wouldn't ring in his voice.

"Yes, sir."

"Now about this magazine of yours. I want you to understand it's not the filth I object to."

" 'Filth'?"

"Your many allusions to fornication," the Dean Reverend said. "A boy your age is naturally curious."

"Have you ever been married yourself, sir?"

The Dean Reverend blushed from his collar to his scalp. "My life is not relevant to this conversation."

"Yes, sir."

"As I was saying. The filth is not my concern. Nor is your obvious disrespect for authority. I was even willing to tolerate the theological irregularities in your first edition. That is why I chose not to intercede. Perhaps I should have."

"Sir—"

"But when your inquiries turned to atheist propaganda, which I see now must have been your purpose from the start, you crossed the line between curiosity and sacrilege. *This* I cannot forgive."

The Dean Reverend walked to the front of the desk.

"Tell me, boy: what do you believe in?"

"What do you mean?"

"The thing that gives your life purpose. What is it?"

MacInnes had thought the answer would be obvious.

"Poetry," he said.

"Eh?"

"Man's power to take something ugly and chaotic and turn it into something beautiful."

"Shall I assume you no longer believe in Christ?"

"Christ?" MacInnes said. "Don't talk to me about Christ! Not after what *you've* done to him."

He pointed to the crucifix behind the desk, with its figure

of Jesus nailed to the boards: beaten, bleeding, and pathetic.

"If I believe in Christ," he said, "it's not *him*. No savior of mine just shrivels up and dies when his people need him most. If he was so damned special, why was he so quick to believe his God had forsaken him? That may be Christ for you, but he's no Christ for me."

The Dean Reverend was stunned.

"You blaspheming little snot-nosed fool!" he shrieked. "The church has given you every advantage—your whole life. Taken you off the streets, pressed you to her bosom, fed you, clothed you, given you a chance for the kind of education most boys only dream of. How dare you? How *dare* you?"

He grabbed MacInnes by the wrist and hurled him across the room. MacInnes crashed into the wainscot. The Dean Reverend took off his suit coat and found his wooden paddle. His face was bright red, and a gob of spittle stained the corner of his mouth.

"Loosen your trousers and hold on to the rail."

MacInnes did so just to spite him.

"We'll recite the Lord's Prayer."

"Go to hell."

The first crack of the paddle took the wind from his lungs.

"Our Father, Who art in Heaven—"

"You dirty bastard."

The second crack of the paddle raised blisters.

"—hallowed be Thy name. Thy kingdom come—"

"Do you even have a soul? Have you ever loved anything?"

The third crack broke the skin.

"—Thy will be done, on Earth as it is in Heaven . . ."

Roger and Daphne listened to the carnage from the Dean Reverend's outer office. The Dean Reverend uttered his prayer time and again. His voice grew hoarse, the blows grew more violent. It seemed the beating would go on forever.

"Why?" Daphne said. "What's the point?"

"There *is* no point," Roger said. "It's personal now."

"Give us this day our daily bread . . ."

Daphne was in tears. "Why doesn't he stop?"

"But deliver us from evil . . ."

An hour later, it seemed, MacInnes walked through the door.

"That was fun," he said with a smile.

Then his eyes rolled back, and he crumpled into their arms.

"Oh, God!" Roger said. "Help me carry him."

Dusk had fallen, and they shouldered MacInnes to the infirmary beneath a jack-o'-lantern sky. The infirmary lights blazed, and Dr. Cornwell had a surgery waiting.

"The Dean Reverend phoned," he explained in the voice of one who knew too much. "He's not totally without conscience."

But even he was surprised by the Dean Reverend's work.

"I haven't seen such a mess since . . . Never mind."

He laid MacInnes belly-down on a table and handed him a rag soaked in ether. "Breathe through this."

Twenty sutures later, he removed the rag and rolled MacInnes next to a window. While the patient lay reviving in the fresh evening air, the physician spoke to Roger in private.

"Your friend's wounds will heal," he said. "But his psyche I must place in your hands. A beating like this does its real damage to the spirit."

Roger shook his head. "You don't know MacInnes."

19

Behold her, single in the field,
Yon solitary Highland lass!

—WILLIAM WORDSWORTH

Dr. Cornwell gave MacInnes some worthless pills (which he threw out the window) and he was forced to treat his wounds with tobacco and the memoirs of De Quincey. After a bit of experimentation, he found that by lying facedown with a bag of ice on his buttocks, he could reduce the pain to a tolerable throb.

Wednesday afternoon he tried to stand up, but Roger and Daphne held him down.

"Where do you think you're going?" Roger said.

"I have an appointment with Miss Waverly."

"Not anymore."

"But I have to see her!"

"You will. I changed it to Friday."

"You spoke with her yourself?"

"Yes."

"On the telephone?"

"Certainly."

"Oh! You should have asked me, chum. I'd have explained how it works. The telephone's a little tricky at first, but after a few . . . All right, what are you two laughing at?"

Friday he returned to classes. His first thought was that he must have missed a lot of material, because Edgar Sykes was blithering on about the "Pince Nez Indians," and MacInnes had never heard of them.

"Of course they lost the war," Sykes said, "the whole tribe being nearsighted like that."

When MacInnes finally got it, he limped across the room and cuffed Sykes on the back of the head.

"It's Nez Perce, you dimwit. And their eyes were a hell of a lot better than yours."

Mr. Constantine, their history master, couldn't help smiling.

"Nice to have you back, MacInnes."

He took a walk in the late afternoon. The Stoney Batter shooting range made its home in an abandoned cornfield, where bent stalks and dry husks whispered in the wind. As he'd hoped, a lone figure prowled the embankment. She wore khaki pants and a houndstooth jacket—a million miles away from Marjorie's flapper garb, and a million times more flattering. She looked capable, that was it, and for the first time he wondered if she'd really needed saving that day by the ruins, or if she'd've stood up fine to Bloxom on her own. He suspected the latter.

"Pull!" she cried.

From some hidden mechanism, a clay pigeon was launched over the field. Laura wheeled her shotgun around as if it were a part of her body. Blue smoke puffed from the nose of the barrel, and thunder echoed across the valley. The target exploded—a perfect shot. Laura pumped the spent shell from her weapon and called for another target. In less than five minutes, she potted ten clay pigeons from the sky.

"That's enough, Sally!"

She turned to MacInnes, who had climbed the embankment to watch. A lock of hair was in her eyes, and she brushed it away. She smiled.

"Good afternoon," she said.

"That was some shooting. You must practice a lot."

"I enjoy it. It relaxes me."

"Do you hunt?"

She made a face. "I went with my father a few times when I was little, but I couldn't stomach the killing. It seemed so pointless."

She took a cigarette from her coat pocket and lit it without waiting for his help. He liked that. He liked the way she inhaled without making a big fuss, or without using a preposterous holder. So far, he liked everything about her.

"I'm sorry I couldn't make it Wednesday," he said.

"Don't be. Your friend Roger—Roger?—he said you took quite a beating."

He told her about the magazine.

"What a stupid thing to be punished for."

Yes, and your insufferable boyfriend helped seal my fate, he wanted to say. Instead, he put his hands on her shoulders and kissed her. It was a gentle kiss, and he broke it himself, but it left both of them flushed and flustered.

"What was it you said at the dance?" she asked. "Something like 'You and I have been lovers since before the dawn of time.' What did you mean by it?"

He thought for a moment.

"When we first met," he said, "did you get a strange *feeling*? As if you'd been searching your whole life for something, but you didn't know what—and you didn't even realize you were searching, until suddenly you found it—and right away you knew nothing would be the same?"

A girl with red hair appeared on the embankment.

"Hullo!" she said brightly. "You must be Michael. I'm Laura's roommate, Sally Fairweather."

"Nice to meet you, Sally."

"Are you ready, Laura?"

"Give me another minute."

Sally winked exuberantly and left them alone.

"I wondered who was launching the targets," MacInnes said.

"We take turns. It's fun."

MacInnes nodded, and then he couldn't help blurting: "When can I see you again?"

"We come here to practice two or three afternoons a week. I don't know why the Hood School can't have its own—"

"That's not what I meant."

She stepped on her cigarette. "I know."

"Does Sally ever go home for the weekend?"

"What you're suggesting is utterly impossible."

"Of course."

"And the fact that she'll be away tonight is none of your business."

"It's a good thing you didn't tell me."

"Isn't it, though?"

They climbed down to the farm road. Sally was already waiting in the Bugatti. Even parked, the roadster looked fast. Laura slipped into the driver's seat and put on her goggles.

MacInnes had never met a girl like this.

"You know," she said, "Trent Bloxom expects me to marry him."

"You won't do it, though."

"Why do you say that?"

"Because you're already falling for me."

"Am I?"

She started the engine and adjusted the gears. The car began to move. MacInnes jumped onto the running board, and they sped down the road together.

"You must be crazy!" Laura laughed.

"You never answered my question!"

The car took a bump, and MacInnes nearly went flying.

"Yes!" Laura shouted. "I felt it!"

Grinning, MacInnes jumped off the car. He watched until the dust cleared and the car vanished over a hill. Then he walked back to campus. He had some preparations to make.

Edgar Sykes walked out of the cornfield. He felt like a scarecrow: dead leaves stuck out of his collar and cuffs, cobs filled his pockets. He'd even been shot! Or if not exactly shot, he'd been pelted with shards of clay pigeon. One of them had nicked his ear!

It had been worth it, though.

MacInnes was going to meet that girl tonight. This was just the sort of information that Howard had sent him out here to find. He wasn't sure what Howard would do with it yet—but if *Sykes* were in charge, he'd hide in the girl's room until things got mushy, and then he'd leap out of the closet and yell, "Who's the dimwit now, MacInnes? Who's the dimwit now?"

20

Numb were the Beadsman's fingers . . .

—JOHN KEATS

Who thundering came on blackest shoe, with strange
pangs flashing along his brow? The wandering outlaw
of his own dark mind . . .

An hour before curfew, MacInnes sneaked out of Craxton
House in the darkest clothes he owned. With hardly a glance
behind him, he slipped into the woods that ran between the
two campuses.

Moonlight filtered through the treetops and lent the
woods the sort of Arthurian luminescence one needed for a
quest like this. For hours, it seemed, he splashed through
streams, tramped through thickets, scrambled over broken
walls. The woods were madness—madness! Just when he was
sure he'd gone the wrong way, he staggered through the fo-
liage onto a wide, grassy lawn. On the other side was a familiar array of old stone buildings.

He'd never visited the Hood School, but he recognized
every detail from the ice sculpture he'd studied at the Grand

Cotillion. He made a beeline for the dormitory and promptly fell on his face. With his eyes in the grass, he saw why. The lawn had been mined with croquet wickets. Here and there lay discarded mallets and parti-colored balls. The Hood School girls were crafty, all right. They'd foreseen his arrival and booby-trapped the place!

Somehow he made it across without crippling himself. All that remained was to get inside. Simple. Or was it? He checked the front door. It was locked. And if he started banging on windows at random, he would certainly arouse suspicion.

Shouldering his rucksack, he circled the building. At last he spotted an open window on the third floor. Even better, it was a *lavatory* window. At this time of night, he could enter it safely. A nearby tree limb would take him right to it.

He started to climb. He was no stranger to work, but the last two months at Stoney Batter had softened his hands, and the tree bark chewed his palms. Spiders and other creatures scurried into his clothes. Every inch of his body began to itch. He recalled an old Buddhist trick and banished the itching from his mind. It didn't work.

He came to a fork in the tree and shimmied onto the limb. The window lay dead ahead. He crawled through twigs and snarls. The window came closer. A hungry bird pecked at his fingers. He swatted it away. At the end of the limb, he hesitated. The gulf between him and his goal was a good six feet. From the ground, it hadn't looked that far. No matter—he would jump. He rose to an awkward crouch and bounced the limb. He hoped the tree's natural elasticity would give him the boost he needed. The limb creaked but did not break. He was almost there. One, two, three . . .

No doubt it was the added weight of the rucksack that ruined the maneuver. His aim was fine. His altitude was the catastrophe. His fingertips just grazed the windowsill before he dropped into the garden below.

"Oof!" he gasped as the air was slammed from his lungs. He wondered if he'd torn his sutures.

He pulled himself out of the peat moss and sought a new plan. What he found was a bamboo pole half hidden in the shrubbery. He dug it out and gave it a little shake. It seemed a bit flimsy, but it was very long, and he thought it might work.

He stood away from the building, gripped the pole in what he hoped was the correct manner, and started running. He could only guess at the correct distance. He planted one end of the bamboo in a gopher hole and shot into the air. The sensation was amazing—as if some giant fist had snatched him from the earth and borne him aloft. He traveled along a geometrically perfect arc—Roger would have been impressed—before crashing into the wall and dropping into the peat moss *again*.

By now his entire body must be broken.

"Psst! Hey, you!"

MacInnes nearly soiled his trousers. He lay in the dirt and hoped he was dreaming—or the voice had meant someone else. No such luck. Against the awful blackness that surrounded him, a face appeared with an even blacker complexion.

"Miss Dubois!"

"Keep your voice down!"

"What're you doing here?"

"You're in love, aren't you?"

"Well—"

"You're trying to see the Waverly girl, aren't you?"

"Well—"

"Well, nothing! I'm going to help you do it!"

She fished inside her matronly bosom and produced all kinds of strange items: a pouch of herbs, a rabbit's foot, a mummified lizard, two small vials of an odd green liquid, and finally an ancient key. She handed him the key and gathered up the rest of her trinkets.

"Use this on the back door," she instructed. Then she told him how to find Laura's room.

MacInnes was baffled. "Why—?"

She grinned with a mouthful of horsey yellow teeth.

"Let's just call it Christian charity."

"But I'm not even Christian."

She laughed. "Neither am I!"

The key opened the back door without a whisper. MacInnes crept through a lobby adorned with velvet chairs and sterling tea sets. A pair of attack dogs slept by a grandfather clock. He took off his shoes and climbed the oak staircase in his stocking feet. He approached Laura's door with his heart in his head. His mouth was dry. What if her room was locked? What if the dogs beat him to it? What if Laura rejected him?

Never mind.

He opened the door, slipped inside, and stood panting in the dark. She lay in bed beneath the window, surrounded by pillows, her cheeks washed in moonlight. Her breast rose and fell. The other bed in the room, Miss Fairweather's, was empty.

Working quietly, so as not to wake her, MacInnes prepared the love feast.

On her dressing table he lit candles and incense. On the floor he sprinkled rose petals. On a lacquered tray he arranged fancy chocolates, candied ginger, myriad fruits, exotic nuts, and two cruets of Japanese plum wine that he'd been hoarding for an occasion like this.

Satisfied, he sat on the foot of her bed and strummed a small guitar in the ancient Phrygian mode. To the music's rhythm, he composed a small poem:

Raven's wing and midnight cheek—
My timeless love o'erbrims my cup.
My heart is numb, my flesh is weak.
Arise, sleeping goddess, and sup.

Laura's eyelids fluttered open.

"Michael?" she said. "Is it really you?"

MacInnes laid down his guitar and knelt by her side. Taking her hand in his own, he said, in all seriousness: "I've come for you, my darling."

She sat up and yawned. "What time is it? I'm starving!"

"I've brought you a midnight snack."

He fed her slices of tangerine and thought he would die when her teeth crushed the pulp and her mouth wet his fingers.

"Where did you get all this stuff?" she said.

"Here and there, around the square."

"I suppose you've done this for Marjorie dozens of times."

He froze.

"Who?"

"Marjorie Culpepper? Your girlfriend?"

"Marjorie," he said decisively, "is *not* my girlfriend."

"But I saw you at the dance."

"She trapped me while I was looking for you. And then things got confused."

"She seems to think it's more than that."

"Well, she's lying. Or a lunatic."

"The consensus around here is that she's both."

MacInnes laughed. "That's ironic. She's got *you* pegged as a snob."

"She thinks anyone's a snob who won't join that petty little clique of hers."

"The Galoshes Quartet?"

"You've met them?"

"Unfortunately."

He took both of her hands in his own. "Laura, I promise you. Marjorie's nothing to me. This is the first time I've even been to your campus. I'm here because of you. Because I love you, and I'd risk life and limb to prove it."

The confession seemed to startle her. "Really?"

Instead of saying anything more, he kissed her. He kissed her long and hungrily, the way he'd wanted to for as long as he could remember. He kissed her lips, her neck, her ears, her eyes. He was a sheik beneath Arabian skies.

"Michael—before we go on—I have to tell you something."

"Can't it wait?"

"No. You see, I'm still—that is, I've never . . ."

He'd expected this moment. "Do you want to stop?"

"That's just the thing," she said. "I *don't* want to stop. I'm frightened—but it's wonderful, too. I've never felt this way."

"Not even with Bloxom?"

"Almost—a few times—but then I always got bored."

"No wonder he's so frustrated."

"I told you it wasn't his fault."

"And you're not bored with me?"

Now it was her turn to laugh.

"After you set up this bizarre fantasy? Michael MacInnes, I don't think I shall ever be bored with you!"

21

Fierce-throated beauty!
Roll through my chant with all thy lawless music.
—WALT WHITMAN

Roger and Daphne sat on the widow's walk. The air was cold, and they kept their fingers intertwined. Since the night of the cotillion, they hadn't once mentioned what had happened between them. Yet here they sat—alone, together, on the brink of a huge decision. Roger wondered what to do.

"How many are there?" Daphne said. "The stars, I mean."

"Trillions," Roger answered. "Or more. Nobody knows really."

"And if each of them has eight planets—"

"They won't, though. Some of them won't have any."

"Half, then," Daphne conceded. "A third. Even a tenth—"

"It's still a lot of planets."

"And some of them will have people—maybe not like us, but they'll be intelligent, they'll have souls."

"Probably. Where're you going with all this?"

"With so many others, I can't help wondering why God's so interested in us. Are we really that special?"

Roger smiled. "You've been listening to MacInnes."

"Have I?"

"Admit it. You don't believe in God any more than I do."

"I *want* to believe."

"But you can't."

"No." Daphne shook his head. "I can't."

It was the sort of confession that might lead to another. So say it, Roger thought. Holding hands in the dark was child's play. You could pretend it wasn't happening. But talking about it—that would make it real.

"Daphne—"

He was interrupted by a pounding at the door.

"Hello?" It was Mr. Hamilton-Smythe. "MacInnes, you there?"

They scrambled through the window. Daphne buried himself in MacInnes's bunk, and Roger went to the door.

"Ah! Legrande," the old man huffed. "I need to speak to your roommate."

"He's asleep."

"What!"

"Curfew rang an hour ago."

Mr. Hamilton-Smythe looked at his watch. "By Jove, it did. No matter. This will only take a second."

Roger led him up the tower stairs.

"I love the way you've fixed the place up, by the way." He pointed his cane at Roger's laboratory. "I won't ask about *that*, however. Boys! Always into something. Is this his bunk?"

Roger nodded.

"MacInnes, you awake?"

Daphne moaned beneath the covers.

"Speak up, man, you sound delirious!"

"It's the medication Dr. Cornwell gave him," Roger explained. "He takes it to help him sleep."

Mr. Hamilton-Smythe nodded grimly. "He'll be himself in the morning?"

"I guarantee it," Roger said.

"Good thing. MacInnes's punishment starts tomorrow. He's to report to the maintenance chief after breakfast. You got that?"

"Yes, sir, I'll tell him."

"Fine." The old man hobbled down the stairs. "Good night!"

No sooner had the door closed than it was opened again.

"Did you forget something, sir?"

"Quite the contrary," said Howard Entwistle.

"What the hell do you want?" Roger demanded.

Entwistle climbed into the room and snatched the covers off Daphne.

"I thought as much," he said. "Your little friend's visiting after hours. And MacInnes—why, I'd hazard to guess he isn't even in the building. Such a flagrant disregard for the rules."

"You're a fine one to talk."

"Oh, I've already talked."

Roger blinked. "What do you mean?"

"I mean, *chum*, that I know all about MacInnes's tryst with Laura Waverly. And so does Mrs. Vanderlip. We had a lovely chat on the telephone. I didn't mention any names, of course, but she'll figure it out. And when she does"—Entwistle grinned—"it'll be the end of MacInnes, once and for all."

"You bastard," Daphne said.

"Please—my modesty."

"When did you call her?" Roger said.

"A few minutes ago actually. But I wouldn't get any ideas if I were you. The Hood School is miles from here."

"Get out."

Entwistle frowned. "It was only a matter of time, you know. After he pulled that Heretic stunt, MacInnes's days at Stoney Batter were numbered. I'm simply hurrying things along. Doing him a favor, really."

"GET OUT!"

"I'm leaving, I'm leaving. No need to be testy."

Roger locked the door behind him.

"Now what?" Daphne said.

"Come on!"

Roger started hauling pieces of equipment out the window.

"What are you doing?" Daphne said.

"Saving MacInnes, what else?"

"Is that some kind of radio? What's the bicycle for?"

"It's not a radio. Grab those helium tanks, will you?"

"I'm getting a strange feeling about this. Hey—is that a propeller?"

"You catch on fast."

22

O! for a Muse of fire, that would ascend
The brightest heaven of invention.
—WILLIAM SHAKESPEARE

MacInnes and Laura sat naked in bed, feeding each other kumquats and cookies. MacInnes decided that the loveliest part of her body was a small brown mole on her shoulder. It wasn't one of the parts you were supposed to ogle, but it was the one blemish he'd noticed in her complexion so far, and for that reason it made her perfect.

"Are you going to break things off with Bloxom?" he said.

"Yes." Laura sighed. "But I wish it weren't so complicated."

"Complicated?" MacInnes laughed. " 'Bloxom—we're through!' What could be simpler than that?"

"Ooh, you don't understand. Trent and I have known each other since we were kids. Our families go on vacations together. They've assumed for years that Trent and I would get married."

"To hell with 'em," MacInnes said. "Do what you want to do."

"I'm not sure they'll let me."

"So run away from it all. We'll run away together."

"You make it sound easy."

"Because it *is* easy. It's only thinking that makes it hard."

They drank the last of the plum wine.

"What about you, Michael? What do *you* want?"

"I already have what I want."

She blushed. "Besides that."

"Adventure, I suppose. Things to write about. Things no one has ever done before. You know they have mountains in Tibet that have never been climbed? I'd like to climb the highest and watch the sun rise over the rim of the earth. And then I'd write about it so everyone would understand."

"Will you take me with you?"

It was a simple question, but MacInnes felt his spirit soar. "Of course," he said. "It wouldn't be any fun if I didn't."

Abruptly, her entire body went rigid.

"Did I say something wrong?"

"Shh!"

She pointed to the door. MacInnes saw shadows approaching the threshold. Worse, he distinctly heard the chatter of claws in the hall. Claws meant dogs. Dogs meant teeth.

"Laura?" a woman's voice called out. "Are you awake, dear?"

Laura blanched. "It's Mrs. Vanderlip!"

They leapt out of bed. MacInnes snatched up his trousers and threw open the window.

Zounds!

Instead of moss, below him was a cobblestone terrace. If he dropped three stories onto *that*, he'd be killed.

Still, it was worth a try.

"Wait!" Laura said. "I have an idea."

A short while before, Mrs. Vanderlip had received a phone call. When the caller refused to identify himself, she naturally assumed it was a prank. *Good evening, madam. There's a fox in the henhouse.* An absurd idea. But after thinking it over, she decided she ought to investigate.

Now she was glad she'd done so.

"Laura? What's all that noise?"

"I'm dressing."

"Please hurry, dear."

"Yes, ma'am."

Romulus and Remus, the attack dogs who normally slept in the parlor, were sniffing at the door in a frenzy. Their lips were furled back, and saliva hung from their jowls. Something was definitely wrong.

"Laura?" She knocked again. "I'm getting my key, Laura!"

When Mrs. Vanderlip and the dogs burst through the door, Laura was fastening her gown. Her room was clean and tidy and bore no signs of having been visited by suitors. If Mrs. Vanderlip noticed the few motes of soot in the air, she did not say. In fact, she said nothing. She only followed her dogs around the room, peeping under beds, into armoires, into every spot where a boy might hide—and turned up nothing at all. She looked suspiciously out the window but seemed to reject the notion. When she reached for the top drawer of Laura's bureau, Laura knew she'd taken all she could stand.

"Mrs. Vanderlip!" she said.

"Ye-es?"

"That drawer is only six inches tall."

The old lady stopped reaching. "You're right, of course."

"What I am is outraged! How *dare* you march in here and turn my things upside down as if I were a common trollop!"

"But I thought—I was certain—I'm terribly sorry, Laura."

"Just wait till my mother speaks to the board of trustees. Do you have the slightest idea how much money my family has given the Hood School over the years?"

"I said I was sorry—"

"You'll be lucky not to lose your job."

"Oh, dear." Mrs. Vanderlip's hand began to shake. "Laura, you must know this wasn't personal—I was only trying to protect you and the other girls. What if some ruffian *had* gotten loose in the dormitory?"

Laura pretended to think it over. "That would have been unfortunate," she allowed.

"Exactly!"

"I suppose you were only looking out for my safety—"

"You *do* understand!"

Laura escorted Mrs. Vanderlip and her dogs to the door. "It's I who must apologize to you," she said courteously.

"Not at all, dear. We'll just forget the whole business."

"Yes, why don't we?"

"And there'll be no need to bother the trustees . . . ?"

"I won't say a word. Good night, Mrs. Vanderlip."

"Good night, dear!"

The instant the old witch had gone, Laura ran to the bureau. With an unladylike grunt, she shouldered it aside. A section of wainscoting, hitherto covered, was now laid bare. Laura knelt before it, touched a well-fingered spot, and a panel swung open, revealing the entrance to a hidden fireplace.

MacInnes squatted where the andirons had sat.

"You can come out now," Laura whispered.

He squeezed through the open panel and brushed the soot off his clothes.

"Nice trick," he said. "What's it doing there?"

"Every room has one. They were all boarded up when the school changed to central heating. I only hope Mrs. Vanderlip doesn't remember. You'd better run, my love."

MacInnes stopped buttoning his shirt. "What did you say?"

"Er—nothing."

"You do love me!" he cried. "Tell me again!"

"Well, I certainly am fond—"

"Now you make me sound like a puppy."

"All right." She shuddered. "Heaven help me, I do love you."

"I knew it!" He kissed her. "And I love you too. And you'll get rid of Bloxom, right?"

"As soon as I can."

"You won't regret it for a—"

There was another knock at the door.

"Laura? I am *certain* I hear a young man in there!"

"I told you she'd figure it out!"

He was dog food.

"Hey, MacInnes!"

The voice came from outside. MacInnes ran to the window and couldn't believe his eyes. Hovering ten feet away was the most preposterous looking blimp he'd ever seen. Not that he'd seen a lot of blimps, mind you, but this particular blimp looked as if it had been designed by a madman.

The inflatable part, which soared eighty feet into the air, had been stitched together from dozens of bedsheets.

The gondola, if it deserved such a title, was a wooden box fashioned from apple crates.

The engine was a bicycle attached to a fan-blade propeller.

The entire contraption was piloted by Roger. Daphne, at his side, tossed MacInnes a rope.

"Sorry to intrude," Roger said. "But you're about to be discovered."

"No kidding," MacInnes said. "What should I do with this?"

"Pull us in close."

MacInnes took in the slack and pulled the gondola up to the window.

"Laura—" he started to say.

She kissed him. "No time for speeches, my love. Just go."

He climbed into the blimp and pushed off. They immediately began to sink.

"Drop ballast!" Roger called.

"Eh?"

"The sandbags, you idiot! Heave 'em over the side!"

MacInnes and Daphne began chucking sandbags. The blimp rose to a comfortable altitude. Roger was pedaling now, and by dint of a pasteboard rudder, they headed for Stoney Batter.

"This blimp!" MacInnes said. "It's fantastic!"

"All in a day's work," Roger said.

"Day's work, my ass! You were just in time. How'd you know?"

"Entwistle phoned the headmistress—"

"I might've known it was him."

"Then he came by the tower to gloat."

"Uh-oh," Daphne said. "I think we're in trouble."

MacInnes looked behind them. He could still see Laura's room. Mrs. Vanderlip had entered. The two were fighting over something. It looked like a mop handle. Laura fought like a tiger, but the older woman outweighed her by a hundred pounds. She pushed Laura to the floor and wrested the mop handle away. As she poked it through the open window, MacInnes saw that it wasn't a mop handle at all. It was Laura's shotgun.

"Roger!" MacInnes cried. "Pedal faster!"

"This is as fast as it goes, chum."

Mrs. Vanderlip aimed the weapon—

"Don't shoot!" Laura's voice rang through the night.

"You bastards! I'll teach you to molest my girls—!"

BOOM!

MacInnes opened his eyes—he had apparently shut them—and waited for a second shot. It never came.

"All right," he finally muttered. "Who else isn't dead?"

"I'm not," Roger said.

"Me neither," Daphne said.

"You mean the old bat missed us completely?"

"Looks like it."

"Incredible."

MacInnes stretched out on the floor of the gondola and

tried to catch his breath. He was vaguely aware of Roger pedaling the bicycle and Daphne vomiting over the stern. He turned his head and saw that they'd left the Hood School campus and were flying over the woods. The treetops were close enough to touch.

"Say, Roger?"

"Whatzit?"

"Should we be sinking?"

"*Sinking?* No. Definitely not. The first principle of flight is to stay aloft."

"Are we going to crash?" Daphne said. "Because if we're going to crash—"

"Can you see the balloon?" Roger called.

MacInnes leaned backward. High above him, a small section of bedsheet had been torn to shreds.

"I say! Mrs. Vanderlip's a better shot than we thought."

"Drop ballast!"

By now they had sailed past the woods and were flying over the icehouse. MacInnes threw out all the sandbags he could find.

"Hey!"

MacInnes looked down. Mr. Gropek, the iceman, was standing outside his stable, staring at them in dazed fascination.

"Watch where you're throwing that stuff!" he hollered. "And stop being in such a hurry! Buncha damned kids!"

The blimp soared upward, flew level for a while, but slowly began to lose altitude. Fortunately, Stoney Batter was in sight. MacInnes had never been so glad to see the Craxton House tower in his life.

"How much ballast is left?" Roger said.

"What ballast?"

"Tear off pieces of the gondola, then."

MacInnes and Daphne tore out as many sections of wood as they dared. When they were done, what remained was not so much a box as the suggestion of one.

"That should hold us," MacInnes said.

"Not long enough."

"But there's nothing left!"

"There is one item I've been holding in reserve."

"Oh, good."

"Off with your clothes, boys—and don't forget your shoes."

"What!"

"You heard me."

And so they stripped down to bare skin.

"The tower's coming up," Roger said. "I think we'll make it."

"Great!" MacInnes said. "We can land on the widow's walk."

"Oh, dear."

"What is it now?"

"Well—you have to remember, this is an experimental model."

"So?"

"And this is her maiden voyage."

"Quit beating around the bush, old chum."

"There's no way to land."

MacInnes thought it over before laughing hysterically. "All this time, we've been keeping it aloft, and now you tell me there's no way to get it down?"

"I'm glad to see you're taking it well."

"What're we going to do then?" MacInnes said.

"We'll have to jump."

"I think I've read this part before."

"I'm not jumping anywhere!" Daphne cried.

"You want to fly this thing by yourself?"

"I'll jump."

"Good idea. Everybody ready?"

Roger slowed down as they approached the roof, and then he stopped pedaling altogether. The blimp coasted in the wind.

"On three," Roger said. "One . . . two . . . three!"

As they jumped off the gondola, the blimp shot into the sky. The fall was about eight feet. MacInnes absorbed the shock on bent knees. Daphne landed beside him and started to roll off the edge. MacInnes grabbed his arm and held on until Daphne had found a safe purchase on the walk. Then a stabbing pain made him grab his own buttocks. He'd definitely torn his sutures.

Roger was watching his blimp. The wind had blown it past Marshall House and over the playing fields. With no passengers to weigh it down, it flew high and gorgeous—a triumph of Roger's imagination.

"Too bad we couldn't keep it, old chum."

Roger shrugged. "It worked, at least."

"Of course it worked! Got me out of a jam, too. Much as I hate to admit it, your invention really came through."

"It did, didn't it?"

"Can't wait to see the next one."

"Hey!" Daphne said. "Can we take this conversation

inside? I don't know if you've noticed, but we're all buck naked. If someone sees us out here, they might get suspicious."

"He's got a point, you know."

"Very sharp fellow, that Daphne."

23

And this is why I sojourn here,
Alone and palely loitering . . .

—JOHN KEATS

Saturday, MacInnes awoke to an oppressive sense of doom.
His visit to the Hood School had gotten Laura in trouble,
he was sure of that. Just how much trouble, and what he could
do to fix it, he had no idea. Anxious to do *something*, he went
down to the parlor and snatched up the telephone.

"Operator."

"Connect me to the Hood School dormitory," he said.
"And let it ring, please. This is an emergency."

"One moment, sir."

Seventeen rings later: "Hullo?" a girl yawned.

"I'd like to speak to Laura Waverly, please."

His request was met with a very long pause. Not a good
sign. He felt sick to his stomach.

"Are you still there?" he said.

"Yes, I'm here. Did you say Laura Waverly?"

"That's right. It's most urgent."

The girl must have covered the phone, for he was barely
able to make out a series of whispers:

"He wants to talk to Laura!"

"Is it Trent?"

"I don't think so."

"Then it must be the other one. You know . . ."

With a rush and a whoosh, the girl was back on. "Whom shall I say is calling, please?"

"George Byron."

"Okay. Hang on, will you?"

Not knowing what was wrong, he let his imagination run wild. Laura was dead. In a convent. Strapped to a table while the masked inquisitor showed her the instruments of torture.

A new voice on the telephone: "This is Cordelia Vanderlip. How may I help you, Mr. Byron?"

MacInnes wanted to cry.

"Ah, wonderful," he managed to croak. "I'm trying to reach a student of yours, a girl named Laura Waverly."

"I see. May I ask what your business is?"

"I'm a friend of the family, passing through town. I thought I'd pay my respects, you see."

"Isn't it rather early in the day to be traveling?"

"Yes, well, I've a long way to go, and I wanted to get home before the storm hits."

Storm? What storm?

"I see. Well, Mr. Byron, I'm afraid I have some bad news for you. Miss Waverly has left the Hood School."

"Ah. Well, if you could just tell me when she'll be back—"

"Perhaps I haven't been clear. Miss Waverly's separation from the Hood School is permanent. She *won't* be back."

"But—but why?"

"I believe you know exactly why, Mr. Byron—or whatever your real name is."

"I assure you—"

"I've never fired a shotgun before, Mr. Byron. Tell me: was I lucky enough to hit you or one of your confederates? Or did I only damage your zeppelin?"

"Zeppelin! What on earth—?"

"Good day, Mr. Byron."

"Wait! You have to tell me where—"

Mrs. Vanderlip hung up.

Well, he'd done it, all right. Botched up Laura's life so thoroughly she'd be well within her rights never to speak to him again. He stared at the telephone for a good five minutes before it occurred to him that Laura might be home by now. Anyway, he had nothing to lose.

"Number, please."

"Can you connect me to Roquefort, Delaware?"

"Long distance?"

"That's right."

"It'll be a few minutes, sir."

"I'll wait."

More rushing and whooshing. You'd think they were connecting him to ancient Greece. *Prometheus here. Is that my liver? I could stand an overcoat too, if you don't mind. Yes, it gets a bit damp chained to these rocks for all eternity—*

"Operator—how may I help you?"

"Oh, thank goodness! I'm trying to reach Laura Waverly."

"Cyrus and Pamela's girl?"

"I think so."

"A bad business down at that school of hers, eh?"

This was bigger than he'd thought. Everyone alive seemed to know the events of last night.

"Yes," he agreed wearily. "A terrible business."

"I'll connect you right away, sir."

Ring ring ring.

"Waverly residence. Basil speaking."

"Good morning. I'd like to speak to Laura, please."

"Miss Laura's asleep, sir. She had a long night traveling."

He'd found her!

"I understand," he said. "But I'm sure if you tell her who's calling—"

"Miss Pamela said Laura's not to be disturbed. That's until further notice, sir. I'm terribly sorry."

"What if I call back later?"

"I don't think the situation will have changed, sir."

"But I can try, can't I?"

"Yes, sir. Good day, sir."

24

We were the first that ever burst
Into that silent sea.

—SAMUEL TAYLOR COLERIDGE

A solitary figure clanked out of the maintenance shed, scratched his buttocks, and walked over dead, brown lawn. Morning sunlight burst through the junipers and lit up a path across the stubble. Ancient rubber waders, four sizes too big, covered his body from toes to armpits. Saber-toothed rattraps hung from his belt, along with a sack of rotten cheese. A tight coil of hemp nearly hid the bandolier of gas grenades thrown over his chest. The dented doughboy helmet on his head was surmounted by a battery-powered lamp.

A squad of freshmen warming up on the gridiron stared after him in surprise. He looked, one boy decided, like an interstellar gunfighter.

"MacInnes!" someone called to the figure. "Give us a kick!"

"Yeah, Mr. Poetry! Show us how it's done, eh?"

A brown ball shot over the sidelines and hummed through the keen November air. MacInnes pulled it down with his one free hand, noted the muddy laces, the beat-up leather, and shrugged beneath the weight of his gear. He dropped the ball and clobbered it with his vulcanized toe. PFOOM! The ball soared away through the blue, higher and higher, over the heads of the frosh eleven, split the north goalposts, and vanished into the woods without a trace.

"Great Scott!"

"Jiminy crickets!"

Coach Curran had never seen anything like it.

"Now, *that's* what I call a kicker!" he said. "Who *is* that?"

The players closest to him all tried to look busy.

"Well?" he hollered. "Is that boy eligible to play football, or isn't he?"

The tension on the sidelines thickened.

"DOES ANYBODY"—Curran fought for air—"KNOW THAT KICKER?"

"Aw, shucks," a boy named Zebulon Frake finally said. "It's only MacInnes, coach. He don't play nuthin."

"MacInnes, MacInnes—" Curran flipped through a notebook of rosters. "It sounds familiar, but I can't—"

"He's the Heretic, coach."

"That's it!" And then even Curran got it. "Oh."

MacInnes shook his head and walked on. His ass itched like crazy, and his waders made it impossible to scratch.

A familiar snarl drifted over the lawn. MacInnes spotted Mr. Woodknight headed his way—accompanied by Mrs. Vanderlip and those attack dogs of hers. No doubt trying to pick up his scent. Only one thing to do. He fumbled over his shoulder for the war-surplus gas mask the maintenance chief had given him. He fastened it beneath his helmet and felt as if he were breathing through a stack of old bicycle tires.

"Good morning, Mrs. Vanderlip. How d'ye do, Mr. Wood-knight?"

The dogs rolled their yolky eyes at him, twitched their ears, and ducked behind their mistress with their tails between their legs.

Mrs. Vanderlip unfolded a lorgnette and popped it on her nose. "Hullo, young man. What are you supposed to be?"

MacInnes held up his cylinder of poison. "Exterminator!"

"I beg your pardon?"

"He's being punished," Mr. Woodknight explained with a touch of embarrassment. "The Dean Reverend is a strong believer in the power of Good Works to heal the errant soul. For a minor offense, a boy might be asked to polish doorknobs. More serious offenders, like this boy, are given more difficult jobs. The whole idea—and I stand behind it one hundred percent—is that work builds pride, and a boy who takes pride in his school is less likely to act out against it."

"Don't you *beat* them anymore?"

"Oh"—squirming behind his mustache—"we retain the *right*, naturally. But we exercise it rarely."

"I distrust newfangled ideas. How well does it work?"

Woodknight threw MacInnes a menacing look. "Well, boy? Do you take pride in your school?"

"Absolutely, sir," MacInnes's voice echoed through his mask. "I love it here. The Dean Reverend's been a regular father to me. Why, just yesterday I asked his advice on a spiritual matter."

The two adults couldn't believe it.

"You asked—"

"—the Dean Reverend—"

"—for *advice?*"

"Oh, yes. He's really quite warm once you get to know him."

Mrs. Vanderlip cleared her throat. "Was his advice useful?"

"He solved my problem almost before I knew it."

"Remarkable!"

"Not at all." MacInnes grinned. "You see, I was constipated for days after the beating he gave me—couldn't pass a thing—and he suggested cod-liver oil. Cleared it right up, let me tell you. I recommend it highly—if you should ever have a similar problem, I mean."

Woodknight's cheeks turned a blotchy shade of red. "Why, you—you—you're a disgrace! Get out of my sight!" He turned to Mrs. Vanderlip: "Madam, let me apologize! I had no idea this young man had so thoroughly lost his senses . . ."

Eventually, MacInnes plodded up to the sewer vent. Aeons ago, the class of '97 had raised enough money to build a small garden around what would otherwise have been a terrible eyesore. By now, it was all but forgotten. Nothing remained but overgrown boxwoods and a delirium of untamed vines.

And what was this? Standing in the midst of the jungle was Trent Bloxom himself.

"Where the deuce have you been? You're ten minutes late!"

MacInnes double-checked his gas mask. "Is that all?"

"Is that—?" Bloxom sputtered. "I have important things to take care of this afternoon. You could be punished for this."

"I'm already being punished. Or hadn't you guessed that?"

"Oh, you think it's funny now—but you'll see."

"Yes, I'll see," MacInnes agreed. "Bring on the executioner! At least I'll have acted according to my heart—while the rest of the world wasted its time debating the cryptic virtues of bottled soda pop and celluloid collars. 'Gather ye rosebuds while ye may,' for the end draws near."

Bloxom eyed him suspiciously. "What's your name, friend?"

"George Byron."

"Byron? For a moment, I thought you were MacInnes."

"Never heard of him."

"What!"

"I'm a new student. I only arrived two days ago."

"How'd you wind up getting punished so quickly?"

"I got caught up in a prank somehow," MacInnes said. "This chap was selling shower passes, you see, and he asked me to hold his wallet, and the next thing I knew—"

"Yes, yes. I know the scam."

"Maybe it was this MacInnes of yours."

"It wouldn't surprise me in the least."

"Is he a drunkard?"

"Probably."

"A lecher?"

"Definitely."

"Any respect for authority?"

"None whatsoever. He's ruined my life—utterly ruined it."

"Mine as well," MacInnes said. "Why hasn't he been stopped?"

"That's what I'd like to know."

Bloxom eyed him again but shrugged it off.

"All right, Byron, what do you say we get cracking? Help me with that raft. No, no, that big thing. There's a good fellow."

MacInnes held up a canvas bag with CAUTION stenciled over the flap. "This doesn't look like any raft I've ever seen."

"That puzzled me too. But look here: it's self-inflating."

"You mean by pulling this cord?"

"FOR GOD'S SAKE, DON'T!"

With a burp of valves and a great fart of steam, the bag exploded, knocking them both off their feet. A rubber tube jutted into the air and swelled to its full size.

"That was clumsy of you, Byron," Bloxom said. "Now the damned thing's twice as wide as the vent! How are we going to get it into the sewer?"

"Maybe we can bully it through."

They boosted the rusty grate off the vent and maneuvered the raft into its mouth, where it promptly got stuck. MacInnes pushed halfheartedly. It moved a little and lodged halfway down.

"Now what?" Bloxom grew nervous.

"I'll jump on it."

MacInnes climbed aboard and jounced his legs. The raft moved precariously.

"No good," he said. "You try."

"Anything to get this over with."

Bloxom took his turn and jumped for all he was worth. He landed square on the raft, which plunged through the vent easily, and he and the raft vanished altogether. A quiet splash echoed up from below, and a handful of drops pattered into the sunlight.

MacInnes gathered his gear and climbed down the ladder. "Rotten luck, falling down like that," he said.

"If I didn't know better, I'd say you did it on purpose!"

Ten minutes later the raft was meandering through a catacomb of vaulted tunnels and winding black grottoes—Bloxom paddling in the leaky stern, MacInnes in the bow, unconsciously humming. The darkness was thick, but the beam of his lamp lit up buttresses, arches, groins, hips, crumbling stonework, secret passages. The feculent nightmare seemed to go on forever.

What sort of madman would design a sewer like this for a boys' school?

"Where's all the rats?" Bloxom asked nervously.

"Let's take this tunnel to our right."

"What's the matter with the tunnel we're in?"

"No ledges for the rats to nest on."

"Oh. But what if we get lost?"

MacInnes rolled his eyes. "Want me to hold your hand?"

"I'm not scared, if that's what you're trying to say."

"I'm making this turn. Swing your end the other direction."

"What if I don't?"

"We'll go in a damned circle."

They navigated several more turns but found nothing. By now, MacInnes thought, they must be somewhere beneath Marshall House. Behind him, Bloxom was getting squirrelly.

"Do you have to keep making all that racket?" he complained.

"What do you mean?"

"You're humming."

"I am?"

Indeed, MacInnes was putting on quite a symphony, working the many muscles of his face to simulate the various instruments of an orchestra: trumpets, oboes, violins, bells. He brought in tenors and sopranos, baritones and castratis. What little Wagner he knew he bellowed with a bad Italian accent. What he lacked in talent he made up for with enthusiasm, pausing only long enough to wipe the spittle from the lens of his gas mask.

"Hey," Bloxom said. "Do you see something over there?"

MacInnes trained his lamp on a narrow ledge that flanked the stone walls above the waterline. A hundred pairs of tiny red eyes glared back at him. Whiskers twitched. Tiny feet waved. (They *did* like music!) One brawny stallion rose up on muddy haunches and snickered through yellow incisors.

"Er—let's turn around," Bloxom said.

"I thought you weren't scared."

MacInnes pumped his cylinder, pointed the nozzle at a family in the mezzanine—and hesitated. So what if a bunch of rats lived in the sewer? What right did MacInnes have to cancel their opera? What right did the Dean Reverend have to send him on this mission in the first place?

"What are you waiting for, Byron?"

"I'm thinking."

"Think later. They've spotted us. Some of them look hungry!"

"Yeah, but—"

"Kill them, Byron! Kill them now!"

25

He fancies it would be a satisfaction to be run through the body.
—RICHARD STEELE

MacInnes squeezed the trigger, and a spindle of liquid death shot out of the cylinder. The first rats to be hit died instantly. They were the lucky ones. Those who were just grazed by the silver jet rolled onto their shoulders and kicked their pink feet at the ceiling—lips rolled back, eyeballs bulging. The tunnel resounded with horrible shrieks. Most of the survivors took flight. More out of self-loathing than out of pity, MacInnes aimed the nozzle at the wounded and finished them off. Soon the ledge was littered with bodies.

"This isn't turning out the way I figured," he muttered.

"You can say that again."

MacInnes turned around. Bloxom grinned through his mask.

"Better than editing magazines?" MacInnes said in disgust.

"How do you know about that? I thought you were new here."

"The maintenance chief told me."

"He didn't tell me a thing about *you*."

"Guess I have one of those faces."

"Yes, well—just remember who pulled the trigger, Byron."

MacInnes threw his cylinder into the back of the raft. "It's all yours, then."

"But we're not finished yet! We're not supposed to quit until we've been through the whole sewer!"

"You do it your way, and I'll do it mine."

MacInnes slipped over the side of the raft and stood in the shallow stream. The water hugged his legs like cold pudding. The bottom heaved uneasily. The muck was deep—and moved on its own. Leeches maybe. Leviathan's tongue. MacInnes carried his gear away from the raft, into the icy darkness.

"Where the hell are you going?" Bloxom called after him.

"Like you said, we've got a job to do."

"Yeah—but can't we do it together?"

MacInnes grunted and turned down a narrow passage.

The voice behind him echoed dimly. "What if I get lost?"

MacInnes walked upstream. Frothing cataracts spilled out of rusty spouts in the walls. The ceiling grew lower, so that he had to stoop, and he came to a sandbar piled with rubbish: cigarette butts, scraps of paper, even a bloated copy of Dante's *Inferno*. A perfect location for some rat's nest. He flashed his lamp into the corner and watched a red tail slip into a heap of fallen stones. For the next hour, he baited traps. This way, he could do the job without actually having to watch something die.

A gas grenade thudded in the distance.

"Yee-ha!" Bloxom bawled.

Idiot.

MacInnes tramped into another tunnel. A rat came out of nowhere, running straight for him down the center of the passage. She (somehow he knew it was a she) was suicidal. She'd seen her comrades suffer and wanted to end it all fast. Except that MacInnes had left his cylinder of poison behind, and there was no sense setting off a grenade for one rat. He hefted his bait satchel and thought: I'll hit her swift and solid, and it won't hurt so much.

Abruptly the rat stopped dead in her tracks, looked up at MacInnes with sad, brown eyes, and started to cry. It was only sewer water rolling off her head, but in the glow of his helmet lamp, it looked like tears.

He couldn't do it.

Punishment or no, he was through with killing.

"Yee-ha!" screamed a voice at his shoulder, and the next thing he knew, the rat was rocketing out of sight on the tip of a silver spire. Bloxom stepped forward, cylinder in hand. "Gotcha! Did you see that, Byron?"

"You're a hell of a sport."

"Don't give me that. It's all in the Bible. Man's natural dominion over beasts."

"Sure."

MacInnes was backtracking the rat's path. It led behind some cardboard to an old cigar box. Inside were a half dozen fuzzy pink blobs. Noisy ones too: Eep! Eep! Eep! That crazy rat hadn't wanted to commit suicide at all. She'd been trying to protect her babies. And now they were orphans. Like him.

"I say." Bloxom came closer. "What have you got there?"

"Get away from me, you bastard."

"If you're not going to kill them, stand aside."

"Not on your life!"

"Now who's scared?"

Bloxom aimed his nozzle.

MacInnes kicked the cylinder out of his hand. It flew down the tunnel, football style, and splashed into the stream. A murmur of bubbles reported its fate.

Bloxom massaged his wrist in disbelief. "That was school property!"

"Accidents happen. You understand what I'm telling you?"

"You nearly kicked my arm off!"

"Tell it to Dr. Cornwell. I'm getting out of here."

"But we're not finished! I'll be here all day if I have to do it myself."

MacInnes looked for a way out. No longer in the mood for his charade, he pulled off his gas mask and reached inside his waders for a cigarette.

"Hey!" Bloxom came toward him. "You *are* MacInnes!"

"Aw, go away."

"You son of a bitch!" Tearing off his own mask. "What kind of fool do you take me for?"

"That's a tough question."

"I mean, who do you think you are, breaking into my girl's room last night?"

"Is this the same girl you tried to rape in the woods?"

"Of course it is! I mean . . ." Even in the darkness of the tunnel, Bloxom's cheeks turned visibly scarlet.

"And she claims I broke into her room?"

"I don't know what she claims—she hasn't said a word. Poor thing's probably traumatized. But it was you, all right. I saw the way you hypnotized her at the cotillion. You said you were only dancing, but I knew better. And now you've got her kicked out of school!" Bloxom was almost sobbing.

"Look, chum," MacInnes said. "I'm not confessing to anything. But if it's the way you say it is, how do you know Miss Waverly wasn't a willing partner?"

"What are you implying?"

"She may have invited someone into her room. Lovers are like that, you know."

"But she's *my* girlfriend, damn it!"

"They didn't show her the door for no reason."

"But she hasn't said a word, not to anyone. Mrs. Vanderlip doesn't know the whole story. It's a misunderstanding—it has to be."

"Do you really believe that?"

Bloxom shook his head morosely. "No . . ."

He suddenly looked at MacInnes with new life in his eyes. "Sir, I challenge you to a duel!"

"You're joking."

"We'll fight like gentlemen. The last one standing keeps the girl."

"Don't be ridiculous. We've already *lost* the girl."

Bloxom punched MacInnes square in the chest, striking the bandolier of gas grenades with a resounding *thunk*. "Oh, hell!" He brought his knuckles to his mouth.

"There you are: it won't work. Now what say we go back to my digs and scrounge up a bottle of—"

"Shut up! And take off your clothes."

MacInnes frowned. "You've heard the wrong rumors about me."

"I mean so we can fight!"

"You sure you wouldn't rather have a drink?"

"Don't want to use your fists, eh? I knew you'd turn out to be a coward. All right. We'll need weapons."

Bloxom ran back down the tunnel. MacInnes shook his head and closed his eyes. When he opened them, Bloxom handed him a six-foot length of rusty pipe. Bloxom held its twin.

"We'll fight to the death! Winner keeps the girl! Agreed?"

"Aw, come on, chum. I don't want to hurt you."

Vibrations cantered up MacInnes's arm as Bloxom dealt his weapon an encouraging blow.

"Fight back, you miserable cad!" Bloxom hoisted his pipe and let it fall toward MacInnes's head.

MacInnes parried the blast, and the pipe gouged a big chunk of stone from the tunnel wall.

"Look," he said. "You'll only hurt yourself."

Bloxom swung at MacInnes's knees. MacInnes leapt over the whistling pipe just in time.

"Fight back!" Bloxom cried.

He swung again, this time smacking MacInnes's elbow.

"Ouch! Hey, that hurts."

Bloxom smacked MacInnes's wrist, and his whole arm went numb. Despite himself, he was impressed with the idiot's stamina. These pipes were heavy.

"Look," he said thickly. "I've had about enough of this."

"Bastard! Lecher! Defiler of women!"

MacInnes parried another blast, and his pipe shattered into pieces, leaving him without a weapon.

"Aha!"

Bloxom charged. He swung at MacInnes's head, but he must have lost his nerve, for the blow was only glancing.

Still, MacInnes fell over and nearly blacked out.

"You're lucky I didn't kill you," Bloxom panted.

"You're a . . . hell of a . . . gentleman." He struggled to get up, but all his strength had left him.

"Here." Bloxom reached out a hand, and MacInnes tried to grab it. True to form, Bloxom pulled back, and MacInnes was left holding a dirty handkerchief. "I believe that's yours," Bloxom said. "Looks like you could use it."

MacInnes tried to say "Thanks," but it came out "Fig." How frustrating for a poet to be fumbling for words!

"I think it's only fair to tell you," Bloxom added, "that as of four o'clock this morning, Laura Waverly and I are engaged."

"Huh?"

"Her father and I worked it out on the telephone."

"Didn't . . . speak . . . Laura?"

"It wasn't necessary. Transactions like this are made all the time."

"Transashen—?"

"Oh, for God's sake, stop being so naïve. How was an orphan like you going to fit in with the Waverlys anyway? You don't talk right, you don't dress right. You're a goddamned nuisance!"

MacInnes wrinkled his brow.

"Yes, I know where you come from," Bloxom said. "You

might think that love conquers all, but in my world it's a little more intricate. You want some advice? Stick with Miss Culpepper. West Virginia girls don't care who they lie down with—even if they are filthy rich."

Bloxom kicked him in the ribs for good measure. "Ta-ta, 'old chum.' "

MacInnes lay in a stupor for what might have been hours, and when his head finally cleared, he found himself sprawled in the mud. He had no idea where he was, and his lamp had burned out. Fortunately, the sewer seemed brighter than before.

He pulled himself up and walked toward the light. As he came closer, he realized that the tunnel itself was glowing. He stepped into a chamber hewn from solid rock, and the algae-covered walls gave off their own light.

He almost wished they didn't.

On the other side of a promontory, a dead horse stood stock-still in the water, ribs and shinbones jutting through its rotten hide. Through the weird green gloom, he saw broken swords, dented shields, and rusted suits of armor. It was all just lying around, half in, half out of the water, like the relics of some gorgeous quest.

Where the hell was he?

A familiar sound echoed across the surface of the lake: the rattle and squeak of oarlocks. In the distance (how big was this chamber anyway?) he spotted a small rowboat plodding toward him. For a moment, he thought the oarsman was Miss Dubois. But as the boat came closer, he saw that the pilot was in fact a skeleton robed in black, and that the rhythmic sound came not from the oarlocks but from the skeleton's joints as the raw bones clicked together.

The boat came to a rest beside him, and the pilot beckoned with a chicken-bone finger.

MacInnes climbed into the boat. They rowed across the lake.

"Now what?" MacInnes said.

The pilot waved his arm. MacInnes climbed onto the beach.

"Am I supposed to do something?"

The pilot shrugged.

"At least tell me where I am."

But the rowboat had vanished, and the chamber had shrunk to the size of a normal tunnel.

Had it all been a dream? He rubbed his eyes.

In front of him was a stack of wooden boxes. The stenciling on their sides read: ROYAL CANADIAN WHISKEY. He rushed at the stack and nearly lost a fingernail breaking into the closest box. Twelve brown bottles glittered up at him.

Entwistle's stash.

MacInnes had very little practical knowledge, but he did know this: alcohol was highly flammable.

He opened a bottle of whiskey and splashed it liberally over the boxes. He emptied three more bottles the same way. Then he stepped backward. He struck a match and tossed it at the largest puddle.

Blue flame raced over the stash. The boxes blackened and then caught fire themselves. Woodsmoke stained the stonework ceiling.

Inside the burning boxes, one by one, the bottles began to explode. The additional alcohol fueled the flames, and soon all the bottles were bursting.

MacInnes ducked around the corner and waited for the noise to die down. When he looked back, nothing remained but cinders, smoke, and bits of glass.

So what if he'd lost to Bloxom? Entwistle's poison was gone.

26

Did I solicit thee
From darkness to promote me?

—JOHN MILTON

As Craxton-Marshall Weekend approached, a festive spirit settled over the campus. Soon it would translate into a thirst for liquor, and Howard Entwistle wanted to be ready. He opened his inventory ledger (magnificently bound in cordovan leather) and checked it against the merchandise hidden in his closet.

"Edgar," he said, "our supply of libations is depleted."

Sykes, as usual, was doing his calisthenics. "Huh?"

"We're running out of whiskey."

"Oh. You want me to get some?"

"An exquisite suggestion."

When Sykes did not return in twenty minutes, Entwistle began to worry. It was true, his roommate had never been caught. Might the bungler simply have gotten lost in the sewer? Another few minutes passed, and Entwistle began to perspire. Drops of moisture collected under his shirt and rolled down his back like peas. Should he take some sort of action? When at last Sykes burst through the door, he was empty-handed and shaking. Entwistle jumped up—which, for him, was no small achievement.

"Edgar! What happened?"

"It's gone."

"What's gone?"

"The whiskey."

"The whiskey?"

"It's gone."

"Gone? How could it be gone?"

"Broken glass . . . burnt boxes . . . I think it blew up."

"Blew up? Nonsense."

"See for yourself."

"Everything?"

"Gone."

"The brandy?"

"Gone."

"The dirty pictures?"

"Gone."

"A pattern is emerging."

Sykes put a hand on his shoulder. "Are you okay, Howard? You don't look so good."

"I do not feel well."

"Do you want some chocolate?"

"No."

"How about your medicine?"

Entwistle slumped against the wall. His heart pounded like a train. *Take that, fatty!* the voices called from his past. *You fat tub of lard, you deserve to be kicked!*

"Perhaps in a minute," he said.

"It was MacInnes, don'tcha think?"

"Of course it was MacInnes!"

"So what are you going to do?"

What *could* he do? He couldn't exactly tell the Dean Reverend that MacInnes had blown up his stash. Besides which, he should have expected some sort of retaliation. Still, he couldn't just stand here. If Charlie Schlage—or anyone else, for that matter—decided he was vulnerable ...

"It is time," he said.

"Are you sure, Howard? You really look terrible."

"Don't tell me how I look."

Roger and MacInnes were loafing in the tower.

"So how'd you get out?"

"I knew there had to be a ladder nearby," MacInnes said. "So I looked around, and there it was."

"Don't tell me—it led right to the boiler room."

"Sorry, chum. I don't know how you missed it."

"It's not important. What matters is you blew up the stash. I can't wait to tell Daphne."

"Where is he?"

"Reading to Mrs. Hamilton-Smythe, where else? I swear, he spends more time—"

Boom! Boom! Boom! came a pounding on the door.

"Open up, MacInnes! I know you're in there!"

"Word travels fast," MacInnes said.

He and Roger ran down the stairs and opened the door. Entwistle and Sykes stood in the hall. Entwistle's skin shone with sweat. His hair, normally combed back over his head, stuck out at grotesque angles. His breath came short and fast.

"MacInnes—" he started to say, and then he grabbed his left shoulder and sank to the floor.

"Howard?" Sykes said.

Roger and MacInnes looked at each other. What sort of trick was this?

Sykes tore open Entwistle's shirt and placed his ear on the flabby chest. "He's not breathing!" He listened again. "His heart's not beating!"

"Quit goofing around," MacInnes said nervously.

"I'm not." Sykes gulped. "I think he's dead."

"But he's only seventeen!"

Roger put his own ear to Entwistle's chest. It didn't make a sound. He was dead, all right. Unless—

"He's been real sick," Sykes explained. "His doctor told him not to get excited." He looked at MacInnes. "*You* killed him."

"Me? How? I never laid a finger . . ."

Roger ignored them. He was thinking. What was a heart? Just an oversized muscle. Muscles flexed when nerves told them to flex. And nerves were fired by—

"Wait!" he cried. "I can do it!"

He ran upstairs and came back with a hand-cranked electrical generator.

"Mr. Woodknight showed me. It works on frogs anyway."

Sykes was appalled. "You can't treat Howard like a frog!"

"It's the only chance he's got!"

"Show some respect for the dead."

"That's just it—he might not be dead. At least, not yet!"

"Huh?"

Roger gave the generator to MacInnes and held a naked wire to each side of Entwistle's chest.

"Start cranking," he said. "Hard!"

MacInnes turned the handle—slowly at first but then picking up speed. Entwistle's body jiggled obscenely—but refused to come back to life.

"Harder!"

"I'm cranking," MacInnes puffed, "as hard as I can."

"It's not good enough, damn it!"

"Where's that bicycle of yours? It ought to do the trick."

"We lost it saving *your* life."

"Oh."

"Give it to me," Sykes said.

"Why? So you can jinx it?"

"No. I want to help."

Roger hesitated—then nodded. Sykes was twice as strong as either of them, and if Entwistle was going to live, he'd need as much help as he could get.

Sykes plied all his weight into the handle, and the dynamo began to rage.

"Come on, Howard! Come on!"

"Look—!" MacInnes reached out.

"Don't touch him!" Roger warned.

"I thought I saw him twitch!"

Entwistle's eyes shot open. A fat fist closed around Roger's arm, and lightning blasted white through his brain.

"HE'S ALIVE!" Roger yelled. "FOR GOD'S SAKE, STOP CRANKING!"

Mercifully, Sykes did so. Entwistle's fist relaxed, and Roger pulled the wires away.

"Whuh happen?" Entwistle muttered. "What're you looking at?"

"Gee, Howard," Sykes marveled. "You were dead."

"You'll be dead too if you don't get my medicine!"

"Right away, Howard."

Sykes disappeared. Roger helped the fat boy stand up.

"Ooooh!" Entwistle sobbed. "My skin feels like it's on fire!"

"The wires must have scorched you," Roger said. "I might have something—"

"Butcher!" Entwistle screamed. "Assassin! Leave me alone!"

MacInnes frowned indignantly. "I say, old chum. That's no way to talk to the chap who saved your life."

"MacInnes!" Entwistle thrust out his arms, but Roger held him back. "This is all your fault! I had the world in my pocket before you came along! And now . . . Ooh, my body hurts! Edgar, where's my medicine?"

27

O Solitude! if I must with thee dwell,
Let it not be among the jumbled heap . . .
—JOHN KEATS

MacInnes telephoned Laura's house every night for a week; but the damnable butler refused to put her on. Fiend! Toady! On a whim, he called Laura's roommate, thinking *she* might have a way of getting through. But Sally turned out to be as much in the dark as he was.

At last he wrote Laura a letter. It was a maudlin effort, full of anguish and pathos, sentimental quotations, and an impassioned plea not to marry Trent Bloxom: "You would never be happy. Please trust me on this."

He borrowed a stamp from Roger and walked the letter down to the post office. The sound of leaves crunching under his feet filled him with a sense of peace. Smoke twirled out of chimneys, and laundry snapped in the wind. All he really needed was some tobacco, but of course he'd spent his last nickel ages ago.

A horn sounded behind him. He looked around— Laura?—but did not see the red Bugatti. In its place was a collection of mirrors, horns, and miles of glittering chrome. This was no car. It was a jewelry box on wheels. The top was open, and the driver, as luck would have it, was Marjorie.

"Hey, stranger!" she called. "Haven't seen you for a while."

"I've been kind of busy."

"Of course you have!"

There was no trace of irony in her voice, and he wondered if she knew. He figured she must. But did he care? It seemed like an important question, and his inability to answer it troubled him.

"Wanna go for a spin?" she added.

"I thought you'd never ask."

He climbed into a busy interior of leather and polished wood. The dashboard was all buttons and dials. He even helped himself to a cigarette from a built-in dispenser.

"Where to, darling?"

"You pick a spot."

"All right."

She took a scenic route to the top of Mt. Blazzard. She was a surprisingly competent driver, he thought. Even better, she'd left her flapper garb at home, and with the light and shadow playing on her cheeks, he remembered why he'd liked her to begin with. By the time she set the brake at the edge of an overlook, she was the only girl in the world.

They looked at each other and smiled.

"Hey," she said.

"Hey, yourself."

"You can see the whole valley from here." She pointed. "Look, there's your school."

"I've seen it before."

"Come by me, then."

"I'm by you."

"Come *by* me."

Southern hospitality. MacInnes tried to oblige, but the gearshift intervened, and he damned near killed himself.

"Let's move," she said.

"Good idea."

They climbed into the rear of the enormous car and petted in their usual fashion—that is, getting worked up and then stopping at the most inconvenient moment. Such behavior had a tendency, especially when repeated, to leave a chap feeling awkward—but he told himself it was fitting, that in fact he deserved much worse. He was a cad, a cur, a beetle-headed, rascally knave—

"I've missed you," Marjorie said, laying her head on his shoulder.

"I couldn't get away."

"Yes, but she's gone now, isn't she?"

MacInnes gritted his teeth and tried not to scream. "So you did know," he said.

"Of course I knew! What kind of Dumb Dora do you take me for?"

"Sorry."

"Shucks, don't be! I know how men are. I knew you'd come back to Marjorie one way or another."

"And here I am."

"I have a surprise for you, too."

"Oh?" he said warily.

"Mm-hmm. You know that cute little thing you published? What was it called?"

"*The Heretic*?" The lines of communication between the two schools were more established than he'd figured.

"That's right. I sent one to Daddy in New York."

"I thought you lived in West Virginia."

"We have houses all over," she said dismissively. "Now don't interrupt. Daddy was very impressed. He thought some of the poetry was hard to understand—but he said you must be a genius. He wants to meet you."

"What!"

"You heard me."

"In New York?"

"At Stoney Batter! He's an old boy, you know, class of '95. He comes down for Craxton-Marshall Weekend every year, and when I told him you'd be the Craxton House orator, he got very excited. He wants to hear your speech."

He *had* no speech.

"Michael, are you all right? You look absolutely peaked."

"I'm fine."

"Did I do something wrong?"

"Wrong? Gosh, no. You did *perfect*, angel."

Angel? Who said that?

"Oh, thank goodness. I was starting to worry."

He kissed her decisively. "Take me home."

"But it's Saturday afternoon! We have hours—"

"I need to work on my speech."

"Oh." She pouted a moment. "I suppose that's all right."

They returned to the front seats. He grinned like an idiot and kissed her again. Her pout melted away.

"There is one thing," she said.

"Hmmm?"

"You've had your little intrigue—and I forgive you. But as of today, that's over and done with. No more Laura Waverly, no more anyone else. It's you and Marjorie. Do I make myself clear?"

Michael MacInnes, America's first man of letters, shrugged.

"Why would I bother with anyone but you?" he said. And the crazy thing was, he meant it.

He returned to the tower just as a ruckus was breaking out on the stairs.

"Get your stinking hands off me!"

"Daphne, please—"

"Don't call me that! Do you think I'm a girl or something?"

"Of course not," Roger said. "What should I call you?"

"I don't want you to call me anything."

"Can't we at least talk about it?"

"So you can trick me again?"

"That's not fair," Roger said quietly. "You were the one who said we had so much in common. You were the one—"

"Stop it! Just stop it!"

"There's nothing wrong with being close to someone."

"Liar! I don't need to be close to anyone!"

Daphne stepped into the hall and slammed the door—brushed by MacInnes without a glimmer of recognition—and stalked all the way to his room.

MacInnes waited a few discreet minutes before going upstairs. Roger was sitting on his bunk. He was pretending to fiddle with a slide rule, but his fingers shook too much to control it.

"I suppose you heard everything."

"Just the very end."

Roger shrugged. "I should have expected it, really. He never did . . . Things were never the same after . . ." He wiped his cheeks. "It's always like this, you know. No one ever . . ."

He put down his slide rule.

"Anyway"— smiling sadly—"I guess we're *both* alone now. How shall we celebrate?"

"Roger—" MacInnes started to tell him about his Faustian deal with Marjorie but changed his mind. "I have to write my speech."

"Of course."

"I *am* sorry, chum."

"Don't be. I'm used to it."

"Really?"

"No."

From *The Stoney Batter Gazette* (Special Edition):

> Years ago, the Stoney Batter Fathers sought a way to distract their boys from the drudgery of midterm. A variety of solutions (girls, tobacco, games of chance) were proposed and discarded. One solution remained: an interhouse competition, in which the two dormitories would oppose their champions.
>
> Hence the birth of Craxton-Marshall Weekend.

The first events were purely academic: translating passages of Virgil, solving Euclidean proofs, debating the causes of the American Revolution, and so on. In time, athletic endeavors, such as fencing, basketball, wrestling, and squash, have been added to the slate.

But the past has not been abandoned. Among the cerebral set, chess remains a favorite. And, of course, there is the Quintilian Oratory, with which the events culminate.

To be sure, the rivalry between houses has often reached a boil. But all in all, the competition is a reminder of our Stoney Batter heritage, and a tribute to good sportsmanship —the highest of the gentlemanly virtues.

28

If I don't write to empty my mind, I go mad.
—GEORGE GORDON, LORD BYRON

The evening before the events would officially begin, a group of Craxton House boys found themselves walking to dinner. It was a spontaneous gathering, the product of random motions rather than conscious planning, but a spirit of camaraderie emerged anyway. Even Roger and MacInnes, skulking at the rear of the parade, could not resist joining in a halfhearted chorus of the Stoney Batter anthem:

> *High tower above us her pillars so white*
> *Midst red brick and ivy, a beacon so bright!*
> *Et cetera, something, and trumpets so gay—*
> *His truth is marching on!*

"Listen to *that*," a voice taunted from the library shadows. "If these Craxton House faggots were any happier, I'd have to shoot myself."

The herd fell silent and shuffled to a stop.

"Don't they know we're going to trounce them tomorrow?"

These two voices were joined by a third: "Why should they? We've only beaten them three years in a row!"

The shadows surrounding the library were so dark and heavy that the jesters could not be seen. Their advantage was almost sinister.

It was Charlie Schlage who finally stood up to them.

"You fellows think Marshall stands a chance against us?"

" 'Think'?" another said. "We *know* Marshall's going to win."

"Like to put some money on it?"

"Tut-tut, fellow. Gambling's illegal."

"Chicken."

"Nancy."

"Oh, yeah?" Charlie was miffed. "Come say that to my face."

"Don't mind if I do."

Brian Alder and a crew of linemen stepped out of the shadows. Each outweighed Charlie by at least fifty pounds.

Charlie grinned anxiously. "Oh, say there, Brian! Gee, you played a fine game Saturday!"

Alder grabbed Charlie in a headlock. "You're okay, fellow. Are you sure they didn't put you in Craxton House by mistake?"

All the boys laughed.

"How about you, MacInnes?" a new voice called.

MacInnes looked at Roger and shrugged. "What about me?"

A chap clattered sharply down the library steps. He

was wearing a green fedora. Murmurs chased through the crowd.

"Assaulted any young women lately?" Bloxom said.

"I might ask you the same question."

"As a matter of fact, I haven't. I've been too busy writing my speech for the Quintilian Oratory."

"Er—Trent," said one of the Marshall House boys. "Don't you remember? We all agreed that I would give the speech this year."

"And I'm sure you'd do a wonderful job, Biff. But MacInnes is such a damned nuisance, we have to put our best man against him—don't you agree?"

"But the house voted—"

"It's for the good of the house, Biff. You see that, right?"

"Sure, Trent. Whatever you say."

Bloxom walked in MacInnes's direction.

"Poor MacInnes," he said. "Your atheist bunk may have won a few supporters around here"—gesturing at Roger—"but it hasn't fooled me, and I assure you it won't fool the oratory judges."

He stood with his arms akimbo, as if daring MacInnes to take a swing at him. "I beat you once," he said. "And I'll beat you again."

"You just might," MacInnes said. "Then again, you might not. You see, your real talent lies in bullying people—especially when they think they owe you something. You might not do so well in a fair contest. In fact, you might just fall on your face."

Bloxom laughed uproariously at this, and MacInnes realized he was drunk.

"Spoken like the good man that you are. Let's hope you speak as well on Sunday."

"I will, Bloxom. You can count on that."

A vague signal moved through the crowd, and they all resumed walking to dinner.

"Oh, Bloxom . . . ?"

"What now, MacInnes?"

"Just to set the record straight: I've beaten you *twice*."

Mr. Hamilton-Smythe wrung out his washcloth and replenished it with warm, soothing water. He drew the cloth across Elizabeth's face and gave Daphne silent thanks. Every day she seemed more alert, more like her old self, as if she were just on the verge of springing out of her chair and fixing a pot of tea. It really was a miracle.

He finished her bath and took the washbasin into the kitchen. When he returned, he carried her nightclothes. He gently dressed her and helped her to bed. Every night the same ritual. He didn't mind a bit.

"I have to go out," he told her. "The Dean Reverend's upset about one of our boys. But you know Grimstaff. What *doesn't* upset him?"

He found his coat and cane, and limped across the quad. The Dean Reverend was waiting in his office. Mr. Hamilton-Smythe sat across from him in a stiff oak chair and couldn't help feeling like a naughty schoolboy.

"I suppose you know why you're here?" the Dean Reverend said.

"Your note was rather explicit, yes."

"I was shocked to learn MacInnes will be speaking in the oratory. I assume the *Gazette* is not in error?"

"Oh, it's true, all right."

"And this was your idea?"

"I was the one who asked him, yes."

"Then let me ask you this: What the devil were you thinking?"

"Now, Dean Reverend, I realize—"

"Have you forgotten *The Heretic*?"

"No, sir."

"Have you forgotten what a bundle of smut and blasphemies it was?"

"Well, I wouldn't exactly characterize—"

"Have you forgotten that you gave me your word of honor such a thing would never happen again?"

"That's not exactly—"

"Speak up, damn you!"

"What I promised was that MacInnes would never print another issue of *The Heretic*. To my knowledge, he has not."

"But to let him give a public address? He'll make a shambles of it—a mockery. What guarantee do you have that he won't go off on some obscene, godless tirade?"

"None."

"Have you at least reviewed a draft of his speech?"

"Well—"

"For God's sake, Jeremy. You've licensed him to say anything he wants. Can't you see how dangerous that is? Everyone who could affect the future of Stoney Batter will be attending the oratory. Alumni—parents—the board of trustees. If that lunatic says the wrong thing, the damage could be irreparable. I simply can't take the risk."

"What do you mean?"

"I want you to find another speaker."

"But I can't! It's too late."

"It's never too late."

"Then I refuse."

The Dean Reverend's eyes bugged out. "You *what?*"

"Oh, I know you think I'm a doddering old fossil. But let me tell you one of the few things I've learned in my years. The true educator doesn't distribute truth; he *searches* for it. If we don't give MacInnes—or any other boy—the opportunity to take chances and make mistakes, then what have we given him? Look around, Dean Reverend. The changes in our lifetime have been startling. Radio, telephones, widespread literacy. We've learned the secrets of the atom. We're probing the secrets of the mind. And we've only begun. In twenty years, our truths about history and science will be obsolete. If they're all we teach, we'll have given our boys nothing. But if we teach them how to *explore*—we'll have unlocked the universe. Let MacInnes speak. Give him his chance to learn."

"I admire your convictions. But I have a school to run."

"Do as you must. But I won't be a party to censorship."

The Dean Reverend scowled. He snatched up a pencil and broke it in half. Wood chips flew across the room.

"Do you feel strongly about this?" he finally asked.

Mr. Hamilton-Smythe nodded. "Very."

"Could you at least *read* the speech before he gives it— just to make sure he doesn't embarrass the school."

"I could manage that."

The Dean Reverend looked uncomprehendingly at the pieces of pencil in his hands.

"All right, Jeremy. I'll let the boy speak. But let me warn you, at the first sign of trouble . . ."

MacInnes was squatting on his batik pillow, a pad of paper in his lap, filling page after page with hieroglyphic scrawl. He was onto something this time, quintessential MacInnes: a fiery indictment of rules, fashions, shallow thinking, sexual oppression—in short, everything that had gone wrong with the world since the Puritans had started mucking things up. It was easily the best thing he'd written in his life, and if Marjorie's father—

Marjorie. Damn. Every time he thought of her he got sick to his stomach, and he really didn't understand why. Laura was gone. Out of his life. He'd tried every way to reach her, and nothing had worked. Marjorie, on the other hand, was right down the road. She wanted to see him, and she didn't mind petting. If she helped him get published—where was the harm in that?

Across the tower, Roger fed a nugget of coal to the stove and poked up the fire.

"Horrible," he muttered. "It's just horrible."

"What is?"

"We must have the draftiest room on campus."

MacInnes nodded sympathetically. "Daphne'll come around. I'm sure of it."

There was a knock on the door.

"See? That's probably him now."

It wasn't, though. It was Mr. Hamilton-Smythe. He climbed the tower stairs and spent a few moments catching his breath.

"I've just met with the Dean Reverend," he said.

"Did he beat your ass too?"

"Near enough. He told me to remove you from the oratory."

"What!"

"But that's not fair!" Roger cried.

"Relax, boys, it's all right."

He explained the arrangement.

Reluctantly, MacInnes held out the latest draft of his speech. "You're not going to like it."

"On the contrary. I love it already."

"You're not going to read it, then?"

"No."

"But I thought . . . you just said—"

The old fellow grinned.

"MacInnes, I owe you an apology. When the Dean Reverend threatened you, I should have championed your magazine. I didn't, and I'm sorry."

He limped back to the stairs.

"You make your speech," he hollered over his shoulder. "Tell 'em anything you want!"

From *The Stoney Batter Gazette* (Special Edition):

Craxton-Marshall Weekend is in full swing, and at the end of Day One, Marshall House commands a solid advantage. Under the leadership of Brian Alder, the venerable dormitory beat Craxton House at football, 56 to 2. The Marshall wrestling team won a similar conquest, though an individual victory was claimed by Craxton strongman Edgar Sykes. Marshall's Robert "Bones" Evans won the Mah-Jongg crown for the third straight year, while Roger Legrande of Craxton House was the surprise winner in chess.

Tomorrow's basketball game promises to be exciting.

Of course, the event everyone's waiting for is the Quintilian Oratory. A last-minute substitution will bring Marshall's Trent Bloxom back to the podium, where he will face newcomer Michael MacInnes. When asked if there was any truth to rumors that he and MacInnes were embroiled in an "extramural rivalry," Bloxom would say only, "MacInnes is a sharp opponent, and I look forward to this challenge as I would to any other."

The oratory will be held at 3:00 p.m. in the chapel, after which the Dean Reverend will announce the winning house.

29

He who fights monsters should take care
that he does not in the process become one.
—FRIEDRICH NIETZSCHE

Howard Entwistle attended none of the events. He followed none of the reports, he heard none of the gossip. He did not even know who was winning. His beloved Craxton House meant nothing to him now. His proctorship meant nothing. School meant nothing. All that mattered now was revenge.

He knocked on the door. Power flooded his veins.

"No one's here," Sykes said nervously. "Let's go, huh?"

"On the contrary. We know for a fact that someone *is* here."

"Yeah, but she's a dummy. It doesn't feel right."

"Relax, Edgar. Our quarry will be here soon. He reads to her every afternoon at this hour."

"Yeah, but the speech thing is starting soon."

"He'll be here, Edgar. Trust me." He opened the door and stepped inside. "You see? It's unlocked. He's expected."

Mrs. Hamilton-Smythe looked at them from her chair. A

paisley blanket covered her knees. Her expression wasn't nearly as hollow as Entwistle remembered, but that proved nothing.

"You don't mind if we wait?" he asked.

She blinked.

"I thought not. There isn't much left of your mind, now, is there?"

He smiled at his little pun and walked around the apartment, distastefully noting the ancient furnishings, the faded fabrics, the crumbling books, the portrait of a much younger Mrs. H. squinting into a camera. A heap of cotton diapers rested on the sideboard. Of course—she was incontinent. She was probably sitting in a puddle of urine right now.

"Howard," Sykes said, "I don't think you should be looking at their stuff. Especially not with her watching."

"You mean the 'dummy'? Even if she can understand, she can't tell anybody."

"It's just not right. It's dirty somehow."

"Oh, Edgar. Have our talks had so little impact on your moral compass? My being here is right because I choose it to be right."

"Yeah, but—"

"Silence. There is no 'Yeah, but.' There are only Yes and No. I choose Yes. Do I make myself clear?"

"Yeah. I mean, no. I mean, gosh, Howard, I haven't understood a word you've said since we came back to school. You're not your old self. It's the morphine, I think. And your heart . . . well—"

"You no longer want revenge?"

"I just don't think this is the way to get it. I'm ashamed to

224

be here. If Mr. H. came back right now, I don't know what I'd do."

"He's not going to come back."

"That's not my point."

"Go, then," Entwistle said. "I don't need you."

"That's not true."

"You're a convenience, Edgar, nothing more. Beat it. Get lost."

"Come with me. We'll go have some chocolate."

"The time for chocolate is past. My destiny approaches."

They stared at each other, and then Sykes left. The fool.

"Well, then," Entwistle said to the woman in the chair. "It's just you and me. What shall we talk about?"

Daphne really did want to hear MacInnes's speech—but Roger would be there, and he just couldn't face him. Soon he might be able to, but not today.

He went to Craxton House at the usual time and felt a moment of nausea when he saw the Hamilton-Smythe door standing ajar. Mr. H. must have left in a hurry.

"Hullo?" he said. "Anyone home?"

"Come in," said Howard Entwistle.

Daphne stared into the mouth of a black revolver.

"Jesus!" he said. "Is that thing for real?"

"Shall we test it and see?"

"Nnn!" Mrs. Hamilton-Smythe said, and Daphne didn't know whether to be sick or rejoice. As far as he knew, it was the closest she'd come to regaining her speech.

"What have you done to her?" he cried.

"Relax. Injuring dummies is not on today's agenda."

"I swear to God—if you hurt her in any way, I'll—I'll—"

"Stammer at me?" Entwistle chuckled.

"What do you want?"

"We're going upstairs—to the tower."

Daphne looked at Mrs. H. rocking in her chair. She was trying to stand up. The effort flushed her cheeks.

"Nnn nn!" she said. "Nnn nn!"

"Come along," Entwistle said.

"In a minute."

"You forget who's in charge."

"Aren't I entitled to some last words or something?"

"Sentiment!" Entwistle shook his head. "Be quick about it."

Daphne knelt in front of Mrs. Hamilton-Smythe. "I'm sorry you had to see this," he told her. "I have to go upstairs now. This guy's probably going to kill me."

"Nnn?"

"I'm not sure if I've helped you," he went on. "But I'd like to think I have. It's really meant a lot to me. I just wanted you to know that."

"Nnnnn."

"Are you finished?" Entwistle said.

"Yeah."

In the tower, Entwistle picked up a tennis racket and swung it like a wrecking ball. He smashed Roger's laboratory— beakers, test tubes, pipettes, bottles. Then he turned to MacInnes's stuff—the busts of Keats and Byron, the candles, the incense. Chemicals oozed together and reacted on the floor. Fumes filled the air. Daphne coughed. His eyes watered and burned. By now, the tennis racket hung in pieces, like a broken marionette. Entwistle looked around for something else to ruin.

"Books!" he gasped.

He thrust his gun into the pocket of his suit coat and ripped the pages out of every book in sight.

Daphne saw the opportunity. Entwistle loomed between him and the door, but it would take him at least four seconds to retrieve the revolver. Daphne thought he could just make it.

"You see?" Entwistle roared. "It was all an illusion!"

Daphne slid toward the nearest window.

"His poetry—his dreams—all gone!"

Daphne moved a hand slowly to the window latch.

"And when he finds your dead body—"

Daphne hoisted the window and climbed over the sill.

Entwistle looked up. "Hey," he said. "Where do you think you're going?"

Roger left the gymnasium. Marshall House had won the basketball game, but the scores were still close enough that if MacInnes won the oratory, Craxton would win the competition. He headed toward the chapel and wondered if he'd be allowed to go behind the altar to wish MacInnes luck. He would never know for sure what changed his mind. A voice in his head seemed to urge him to go home. It beckoned him to Craxton House. He walked there in a trance.

What he found was quite real.

Mrs. Hamilton-Smythe lay in the middle of the vestibule.

"Oh, my God," he said.

He crouched over her and wondered what to do. Her cheeks were white, and her breathing was shallow. Had she somehow crawled here by herself? He touched her shoulder, and her eyelids snapped open.

"Are you all right?" he said stupidly.

Her lips moved. She wanted to tell him something.

"What?" He bent closer. "Say that again?"

"Daphne," she sighed. "Upstairs. Gun."

Roger understood at once. The stairwell rang as he took the steps two at a time. The tower door was open. He ran up to his room and gaped at the destruction.

"Christ."

Through the open window he beheld two figures on the roof. If Entwistle was in fact armed, Roger would need a weapon of his own. He grabbed an umbrella (for all the good it would do) and climbed outside as quietly as he could.

Daphne stood like a condemned man at the end of the widow's walk. His back was to the rail. No way out. Entwistle stalked him with a gun in his hand. He looked like a Chicago mobster—or a parody of one. He walked closer to Daphne. He had no idea Roger was behind him, and that was just fine. Three more steps and the fat boy would find an umbrella handle buried in his skull.

"Wait!" Daphne cried. "He's got a gun!"

It was an honest mistake.

Entwistle turned, pulled the trigger, and the gun literally exploded in his fist. Shoddy maintenance. Blood and shrapnel flew in every direction. The bullet itself shredded Roger's earlobe. Entwistle flung the revolver away. His hand was a mess.

It all happened terribly fast.

And then Roger was falling backward. The safety rail disintegrated under his weight, and he tumbled down the slate-shingled roof.

"Roger—!"

He splashed into the rain trough with a screech of stressed metal. It was the sort of trough you found on tall buildings, as wide and deep as a canoe. The icy water soothed his ear, but his legs were so cold they hurt. He sat up, dripping, and reached for the adjacent roof.

It wasn't there.

A section of rain trough had broken free and swung away from the building, taking Roger with it. The downspout beneath him was the only thing holding the structure up. He tried crawling through the water to the opposite corner, where the rain trough was still attached, but the slightest motion caused the whole arrangement to swing further into space.

"Hello, there," Entwistle said jovially. "Like some help?"

He slid down the roof on his massive rump and wedged his fingers beneath the slates to keep from sliding further. Help turned out to be the last thing on his mind. He started kicking at the rain trough. Roger felt every blow in his ear. The trough moaned. Nails popped out of the woodwork. Welds burst, metal tore. In a second, the rest of the trough would break loose.

And then he'd be done for.

30

She loosed the chain, and down she lay;
The broad stream bore her far away.
—ALFRED, LORD TENNYSON

MacInnes was rehearsing his speech in the chapel vestry: "And what are the fruits of this so-called progress? Armored landships and mustard gases that double the convenience of killing a man? Telephones that eliminate the need to meet our loved ones face-to-face? Radios that make it possible to digest the complete works of Blake without having to read a single—?"

The door crashed open behind him.

"MacInnes—thank God."

"Go away, fiend! Can't you see—"

"It's important."

He turned around. Edgar Sykes stood in the doorway.

"What do *you* want?" MacInnes said. "Thou stooge of a stooge, thou serviceable villain, thou disciple of doom."

"It's Howard," Sykes said. "He's out of his mind. He's going to kill the little guy."

"What are you babbling about?"

"Howard's going to murder Daphne to get back at you—right now, while there's no one in the house. You've gotta hurry."

"Liar! It's one of Entwistle's *tricks*. He wants me to forfeit the contest."

"I swear. If he knew I was telling you this, he'd kill me."

MacInnes noted the breadth of Sykes's shoulders and wondered at the absurdity of this statement.

"Why should I believe you?"

Sykes reached under his sweater and produced a leather case. Inside were a syringe and two ampules labeled MORPHINE.

MacInnes was impressed. "He's hooked on that junk?"

"At first it was a game. Now he can't live without it."

Sykes threw down the gear and ground it into the floorboards. Glass crunched beneath his heel.

"Now you *know* I'm telling the truth."

MacInnes nodded. "Where are they?"

"In the tower by now. You'd better run."

"Come with me."

Mr. Woodknight surveyed the interior of the chapel from the altar to the great wooden doors. The candles were lit, the pews were filling up. If the Quintilian Oratory went well, it would be a feather in his cap. If not, it would be years before he regained the Dean Reverend's favor.

"No, no, no," he yelled above the riot of the organ. "I said the blue light, not the red one. It's supposed to signify Heaven, you oaf. There—that's the ticket."

Two boys darted down the center aisle, and Woodknight was a few moments identifying them.

"You there! MacInnes! What do you think you're doing?"

"What's it look like?"

"You know the rules. Both speakers must remain in the chapel for thirty minutes prior to the—"

"Oh, bugger the contest!"

"Bugger? I say! Come back here!"

MacInnes and Sykes ran down the front stairs just as the Dean Reverend was climbing them.

"MacInnes!" the latter called. "I want a word with you!"

"Piss off, chum."

The Dean Reverend stared after him a moment and then marched inside.

"I want that boy out of the contest," he instructed. "Do you understand me? MacInnes is not to speak."

"You're too late," Woodknight said.

"Eh?"

"He's already forfeited. Marshall has won."

"How do you figure that?" Mr. Hamilton-Smythe asked. He was leaning on his cane in the transept.

"The rules are clear," Woodknight said. "Both speakers—"

"Yes, yes, I heard you the first time. What do the rules say about substitutions?"

"Well—"

"As the case of Mr. Bloxom illustrates, one speaker may be substituted for another at any time, yes?"

Mr. Hamilton-Smythe limped to the side of the altar, where a boy named Bumpy Claypoole was playing Bach on the organ.

"Bumpy," he said. "How long have you been playing?"

"How long?" Bumpy wiped his spectacles on a shirttail. "Ever since I was a kid, I guess."

"I mean, how long have you been playing here this afternoon?"

"Oh. A couple of hours."

"I thought so." The old man seized Bumpy's shoulder and said, "My boy, you are now the Craxton House speaker."

"No!"

"Yes."

"What should I talk about?"

"Whatever's important to you."

"But who'll play the organ?"

"Forget the organ. The honor of the house is at stake. We're depending on you. Can you do it?"

Bumpy nodded proudly. "I won't disappoint you."

"I say," Mr. Woodknight broke in. "Did you hear a gunshot?"

Mr. Hamilton-Smythe frowned.

"Perhaps it was the Dean Reverend's car backfiring."

"But the Dean Reverend's *here*. We just *spoke* to him."

"Relax, Arthur. You're nervous, that's all."

The problem with the universe was that there was no fixed point of reference—no absolute set of zero-zero coordinates from which all other points made sense. Einstein's relativity proved that.

What if life itself had no moral center?

"Hang on," Daphne called.

Roger looked up from the rain trough. Daphne was still on the widow's walk. The wind had mussed his hair, and he looked very cold.

"Go back inside before you freeze to death," Roger told him.

"To hell with that. I'm going to save you."

"No!" Roger thought a moment and added, "I forbid it."

"Shut up. It's my turn."

Daphne climbed down the roof with Roger's umbrella tucked under his arm. The incline was steep, but by working his fingertips under the shingles he was able to support his own weight. At one point, he tore a shingle right off the roof and started to fall, but he grabbed another shingle and held on. Roger was amazed. With Entwistle's kicks thudding over the valley, Daphne came as close to the edge of the roof as he dared. He looked to Roger as if he were suspended in the air, like an optical illusion, a trick of the light. He held the umbrella by its point and thrust the handle across the void. Roger reached out—

—and missed it by several feet.

MacInnes took in the situation from the widow's walk and realized that the first thing he had to do was stop Entwistle. He ducked under the safety rail.

"Don't hurt him," Sykes pleaded.

"Sure."

He slid down to the rain trough and landed next to Entwistle. Punching the house proctor was like hitting a pillow: all give, no resistance. Entwistle grunted but did not stop

kicking at the rain trough. He'd almost busted it free. Mac-
Innes found the rotted corpse of a bird in the water and
tossed it into Entwistle's face. No reaction.

"You fool!" Entwistle mocked. "I'm invincible!"

MacInnes had had enough of this.

"Don't make me kill you," he warned.

"Go ahead and try!"

"Pretend you're on a swing," Daphne said. "Shift your weight
back and forth."

Roger did so. The rain trough drifted closer to the building, then farther away. Closer, farther. At this rate, Roger
would tear it off the cornice before swinging close enough.
An idea blossomed in his mind, and he yanked off his necktie.
Leaving it knotted, he tossed it out like a lasso and nearly
caught the umbrella handle.

"That was close," Daphne said. "Next time for sure."

"I always figured the damned thing would prove useful."

The rain trough groaned and vibrated. Roger swung his
weight again, harder this time. Too hard—he was falling.
Impossible. He tossed his necktie. The noose tightened
around the handle. He and Daphne pulled together, fighting
gravity, until Roger was certain the necktie would snap, or
Daphne would fall, or the mainspring of time would fly out of
its box.

"Here it comes!" Daphne cried.

"Look out!"

The rain trough smashed into the building. Roger was
thrown onto the roof beside Daphne. He burrowed his fingers

under a shingle and held on for dear life. Behind them, the rain trough broke loose and clattered three stories to the ground.

For a while, things were very quiet.

"I almost had him," a familiar voice said.

MacInnes was sitting on the roof about fifteen feet away. He was alone.

"When it started to go," he told them, "Entwistle turned and stared at me. He had the strangest look on his face. I reached for his hand . . . but he pulled away."

MacInnes choked, only now glimpsing the truth.

"Don't you see? He pulled away on purpose!"

Roger tried looking over the precipice but saw nothing.

"Howard!" Sykes was calling from the widow's walk. "Howard!"

Trent Bloxom's speech was patriotic, pious, and boring. His point was that happiness awaited those who worked hard, played by the rules, and put others before themselves. The audience coughed and fidgeted. Even the Dean Reverend was observed yawning through his nostrils.

While Bloxom spoke, Bumpy Claypoole waited in the vestry and wondered what he would talk about.

He never got a chance to decide.

"Dr. Cornwell!" someone ran up the aisle shouting.

"I say," Bloxom complained. "You're interrupting me."

"For God's sake, is Dr. Cornwell here?"

It happened that Dr. Cornwell was one of the oratory judges.

"Up here," he said from the choir loft. "Is it an emergency?"

"God, yes! I think Howard Entwistle's dead!"

Entwistle lay crumpled on the lawn. MacInnes, Roger, Daphne, and Sykes squatted by his side. The ruined gutter lay in pieces all around them.

"I'm perfectly all right," Entwistle was saying. "Just go away and let me have some rest."

"Aw, Howard." Sykes sniffed. "You can't feel your legs. You need some help."

"Perhaps," Entwistle began, "some of my medicine . . ."

MacInnes looked at Daphne. "What did you do with the gun?"

"I stashed it in a toilet tank."

"And you remember our story?"

"Yeah. But why—?"

AH-OOGAH! AH-OOGAH!

Dr. Cornwell's Model T tore wildly over the lawn, spraying chunks of turf in its wake. (Taking a hint from local farmers, the doctor had fitted the car with tractor wheels so it could be maneuvered anywhere on campus, in any kind of weather.) Dr. Cornwell stalled the engine and leapt out.

"Give me some room, boys," he said. "Did he fall?"

Sykes nodded. He was crying.

"Take my car to the infirmary," Dr. Cornwell told him. "I need a wooden stretcher. Hurry."

"Take your time," Entwistle said.

"Aw, Howard."

By now more cars had pulled up, and the lawn was a swamp of footprints and tire ruts.

"Move back!" Dr. Cornwell said. "And someone get a blanket before he freezes to death. It's a spinal injury, and I don't dare move him until that stretcher gets here."

"There's a blanket in my apartment," Mr. Hamilton-Smythe said and ran off. Even on his cane, he moved quickly.

"What happened?" the Dean Reverend said. "Who can tell me?"

"I can," Roger said. He was pressing his suit coat to his ear to stanch the bleeding. Even so, the whole left side of his head was caked with gore. "Daphne and I were smoking on the roof—"

"The roof!"

"—when the safety rail broke. That's how I hurt my ear. We were both trapped in the gutter. We'd be dead if it weren't for Howard. He heard us calling for help and got us free. Somehow he fell."

"He's a hero," someone muttered. "Howard Entwistle's a hero."

The Dean Reverend's face was very red. "MacInnes, your presence here disturbs me. Why did you leave the chapel in such a hurry?"

"Howard thought I could help. He told Sykes to come find me. They're my chums, after all. I only wish I'd gotten here sooner."

"Did it ever occur to you to ask one of the masters for help? Mr. Woodknight or myself, for example?"

MacInnes looked him dead in the eye. "No, sir," he said. "As a matter of fact, it didn't."

They stared at each other in silence. The Dean Reverend knew he was lying, but he didn't know why. MacInnes barely understood it himself. Entwistle was finished, that was the main thing. The thought of handing him over to the gendarmes seemed indecent.

"We'll discuss this again," the Dean Reverend said finally.

MacInnes nodded and walked back to the scene of the fall. He was met by a young woman and a man who wore a very nice suit.

"Michael," Marjorie said. "I'd like you to meet my father."

"Not now," he muttered.

"He's traveled a long way to meet you," Marjorie said.

MacInnes looked at them both in astonishment.

"I'm very sorry, sir. I just can't talk right now."

"Michael!"

"Marjorie," the man said. "Perhaps this isn't the best time."

"Of course it is!" Marjorie said. "I have it all planned!"

MacInnes walked away.

"Michael, you come back here this instant, do you hear me? Come back here right now or we're blah blah blah . . ."

"Where's that blanket?" Dr. Cornwell hollered.

"Mr. H. went to get one," Roger said. "Here he comes."

"Oh, no," Daphne said. He stood up. "Oh, my God, no."

Mr. Hamilton-Smythe was stumbling toward them. He'd forgotten his cane. In his outstretched arms he bore a paisley blanket. Boys and masters watched his awkward progress, and only slowly did they realize what Daphne had known right away—that within the blanket lay the lifeless body of his wife.

31

I waited three days to get this pen mended,
and at last was obliged to write.

—PERCY BYSSHE SHELLEY

Because of the accident, the Quintilian Oratory was canceled, and Craxton-Marshall Weekend expired with no winner. Bloxom protested, but no one cared. Entwistle went home in an ambulance, a bona fide hero. His spine was broken beyond repair. He would never walk again.

A few afternoons later, Roger and Daphne shared a bench in the quad. They were tired and sad, and they sat with a space between them.

"Do your parents know?" Daphne said. "About you, I mean."

"Sort of." Roger shrugged. "They think I'll grow out of it."

"But you won't, will you?"

"It does seem unlikely."

"And I won't either. It's like having leprosy or being mad. You never grow out of it."

"What if you could? Are you so sure you'd want to?"

"The Bible says it's an abomination."

"Oh, forget the Bible, will you? Entwistle's an abomination. If you can't see the difference—"

"Of course I can! If it weren't for him . . ."

"That's exactly my point. He killed Mrs. H. as surely as if he'd put a gun to her head. And he damned near killed the two of us. That's what I call an abomination. Hurting people. Using them. Selling them poisoned hooch. What you and I had together—what we are, what we feel—no one was ever hurt by that."

Daphne nodded and ran his hands through his hair. He looked at his feet.

"I don't want to lose you," he said quietly.

"You don't have to."

"What do we do, then?"

"Well . . ." Roger grinned. "I've been thinking that what we really need to do is build an aeroplane."

"What?!"

"We can borrow the engine from the Dean Reverend's car."

"Stop it."

"We'll cover the wings with more bedsheets."

"I am *not* listening."

"The hard part'll be assembling the frame. We'll need lumber that's strong but not too heavy. I don't suppose . . ."

Daphne looked up. "Did you say lumber?"

"Why—do you have some?"

"Not me. But I know where I might *find* some . . ."

MacInnes waited for his train at the station. Entwistle had demolished most of his possessions, and the few that survived barely filled a single crate. He cadged a cigarette from a chap selling toothbrushes and pondered his situation. He didn't *have* to leave. The Dean Reverend had failed to crack the story. But he couldn't stay here either. He'd ruined things so badly—Laura, Marjorie, *The Stoney Batter Review*—that he just couldn't take it. Where should he go, then? Back to the orphanage? He'd outgrown it somehow. Chicago, perhaps. Sausage grinder to the world. He was pretty sure they even published magazines there.

He was asking the stationmaster to exchange his ticket when a red Bugatti raced up to the platform and the most beautiful girl he'd ever seen climbed out and started running.

"Give me a minute," he said quickly.

"The next train leaves in five."

He met her by one of the posts that held up the canopy. She wore a gray suit and a simple hat—no flashy beads or silly galoshes for Laura Waverly.

His heart was pounding.

"Oh!" she said. "I was afraid I'd missed you!"

"What are you *doing* here?" he said.

"I go to school here, remember? Just up the road?"

"But—"

"Michael, I've been reinstated."

"That's wonderful! How did it happen?"

"Mrs. Vanderlip changed her mind."

"The board of trustees got to her, eh?"

"Oh, they would have eventually. But I think someone beat them to it."

"Who?"

"Mind you, I only know what Sally told me, so I may not have all the facts. Anyway, it seems Mrs. Vanderlip had a visitor last night. She was dressed like a fortune-teller. No one knows what she wanted, but whatever it was made Mrs. Vanderlip furious. She threw open the door and said, 'Get out of here at once! And take those wretched bones with you!' A few minutes later, she phoned my mother. What do you suppose it means?"

MacInnes started laughing. He hadn't laughed in days, and it felt so good he didn't try to stop. He laughed and laughed.

"What's so funny!" Laura said. "Is she a friend of yours or something?"

"I haven't . . . I don't . . . Oh my!"

By the time he calmed down, his train had arrived and was hissing impatiently. Bells rang, whistles blew—

"Well," he said. "It's sure been nice seeing you again."

"But—" She looked crestfallen. "You're not still *leaving*?"

"How can I stay?"

"What are you talking about?"

"Your engagement to Bloxom."

"My what?!"

"Your—" Was it possible? "You are engaged, aren't you?"

"God no! In fact, I've broken things off completely."

Still dizzy from laughing, MacInnes put his hands on Laura's waist. They felt good there.

"Are you sure? He said he'd worked it out with your father—made it sound like a horse trade."

"My father!" Laura rolled her eyes. "My father's in Europe on business. He doesn't even know I was dismissed from school. Trent was lying, that's all. He wanted to hurt you, I suppose. It makes me even happier to be rid of him."

It was too good to be true.

"Then you're quite unattached?" MacInnes said.

"Well—not exactly."

"Oh."

"I'm attached to *you*. If you'll still have me, that is."

He was so excited he kissed her.

"Now, you realize I'm poor?" he said almost defiantly. "No family—no riches—no future to speak of."

"Who cares about that stuff?"

"Er—some idiot told me you might."

"Nope." She smiled. "So *will* you have me?"

"We'll have each other," he declared—and then he was running to fetch his crate from the porter.

He'd never cared for train rides anyway.

ACKNOWLEDGMENTS

Writing a first novel is a long, lonely business, and I would like to thank the people who encouraged and sustained me. My mother and father stimulated an early passion for language. Gene Munnelly, Paul Murray, Randy Peffer, Tom Post, Brett Singer, Bill Gifford, Jim Sloan, Gene Wildman, Lore Segal, and (especially) Alan Friedman inspired and challenged me to refine my craft. Mitch Fox and Lisa Poirier helped me purge some mawkish excess. John McFadden and Tricia Kowalik nursed me through some very dark hours. Peter Keough, Trudy Lewis, Rob Moore, Steve Tomasula, and the rest of the UH crowd offered sage advice. Clinton Fischer was kind and supportive. My editors, Robbie Mayes and Wesley Adams, transformed my sometimes blurred vision into a magical reality. My wife, Catherine, read every page a thousand times. Strangely enough, my daughter, Deirdre, thinks that writing books is just a part of ordinary life—and perhaps, now that I think of it, she's right. Thank you all.